THE STORY OF IRON

This edition published 2025
by Living Book Press
Copyright © Living Book Press, 2025

ISBN: 978-1-76153-519-2 (hardcover)
         978-1-76153-559-8 (softcover)

First published in 1920.

This edition is based on the 1920 printing by The Penn Publishing Company.

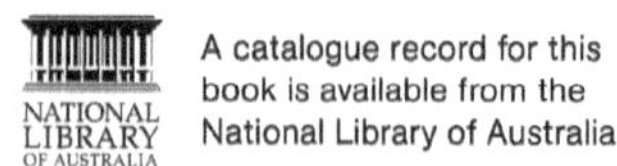
NATIONAL LIBRARY OF AUSTRALIA

A catalogue record for this book is available from the National Library of Australia

THE STORY OF IRON

by

ELIZABETH I. SAMUEL

Contents

CHAPTER I

BILLY BRADFORD

"I wisht," said Billy Bradford, standing, hands thrust deep in his trousers pockets, in the middle of the path, and looking across the broad river at the mountains beyond, "I wisht—"

"William Wallace, come here," called a voice from the door where the path ended. "It's time for you to start with your uncle's dinner."

Billy turned quickly, drew his hands out of his pockets, and in a moment was at the door.

Billy Bradford might stand still, looking away off at the mountains, and wish, but William Wallace was quite another boy. There had been a time when Billy hadn't felt that there were two of him. Then he had lived in the country. That was before the day that his father, hand on Billy's head, had smiled at him for the last time, saying, "Billy, my little man."

Then Uncle John had drawn him gently away, and Aunt Mary had kissed him, and they had brought him to the little house by the river.

1

That was two long years ago. Now, William Wallace had to carry dinners, six dinners a week, to the big foundry, a whole mile away. That was why there seemed to be two of him, one to do errands, and another to think.

"You must be very careful not to fall," said Aunt Mary, as she gave him the bottle of soup, wrapped in two newspapers to keep it hot. Then she gave him the pail, saying, "Uncle John will work better all the afternoon because you are carrying him a hot dinner."

"I shall be glad of that," said Billy, looking up at her and smiling, as he always did, when he was doing anything for Uncle John.

Aunt Mary herself liked to do things for Uncle John, so she smiled back, at least she thought she did; but she didn't know so much about smiles as Billy did. He had been used to the kind that go all over a face and end in wrinkles everywhere.

Billy's smile lasted till Aunt Mary said, "Now hurry, William Wallace."

That stopped his smile, but he settled the bundle a little more carefully under his arm and started on his way.

The day was warm, even for June. Part of the way there wasn't any pavement, and, where there was, it was very rough; so, while he was walking along, Billy had plenty of time to think. He had a great many things to think about, too, for his birthday was coming the very next day, and then he would be thirteen years old.

The thing that was most on his mind was what he could do to earn some money. He was thinking especially about that, because, the night before, when they had supposed that he was asleep in the little corner room, he had heard Aunt

Mary say that the money in the bank was getting very low. Then Uncle John had said, "Sh! Sh! Billy may hear."

June made Billy want to be out in the country. Things were so mixed up that he couldn't seem to straighten them out at all, but he trudged steadily on, because the William Wallace part of him always kept at things. Finally he gave up thinking and whistled hard, just to help his legs along.

At last he turned the corner, and there was the great mill with the square tower almost in the middle; and, at the right, the long, low building with the tall smoke-stack. That was the foundry where Uncle John worked.

Billy went through the wide gate just as the whistle blew; and, in a minute, he could see Uncle John come to the door. He didn't look as if he had been working all the morning in damp, black sand. The men in the foundry said that dirt never stuck to John Bradford. "Clean John Bradford," they called him. Clean and good he looked to Billy, as he stood there in his bright blue overalls and the gray cap that was almost the color of his hair.

"Hot soup, sir," said Billy, handing him the bundle.

"Sure to be hot, if you bring it," said Uncle John, his blue eyes smiling down at Billy. "Might burn a boy, if he fell and broke the bottle, eh, Billy, my lad?"

"Pail, sir," said Billy, his eyes growing bright, until he smiled so hard that he forgot all about his troubles.

Somehow Uncle John seemed to understand a great many things. Even if it was only the risk that a boy took in carrying a bottle of hot soup, it made Billy feel comfortable to have him understand.

"Now," said Uncle John, "we'll go out back of the mill, and have a good talk. Been doing anything this morning, Billy?"

Then Billy told him about the errands that he had done for Aunt Mary and about his hoeing the two rows of potatoes out by the fence.

"Well done, Billy," said Uncle John. "Here's a bench waiting for us. Had your own dinner?"

Billy nodded. Then he said, "Uncle John, do you like to work in the foundry?"

"As to that," answered Uncle John, taking a sandwich from the pail, "I do. It's hard work, and it doesn't make a man rich; but there's something about making things that keeps a man interested. It takes a pretty good eye and a steady hand to make the molds come out just right. They have to be right, you see for, if they weren't, things wouldn't fit together. I like to think that I'm helping things in the world to go right.

"Just why are you asking me that? Can it be that you're thinking of being a man, Billy?

"Something's going to happen to-morrow," he continued, looking very wise. "I've been thinking we'd better celebrate."

"Celebrate!" exclaimed Billy.

"Yes," said Uncle John, nodding his head emphatically. "Just as soon as I've finished this good dinner, we'll go to the office to get permission for you to come to see me work, and to wait until we pour."

"Honest?" said Billy, for he had wanted and wanted to see how iron could ever be poured out of a ladle. "Honest and true?"

"Honest and true," said Uncle John, as he handed Billy one of the molasses cookies that Aunt Mary always put in the bottom of the pail.

"Ready," said Uncle John, putting the cover on his pail.

Back they went to the foundry, then across the yard, and

past lame Tom, the timekeeper, down the narrow corridor to the office where they found the young superintendent at his desk.

"Why, Bradford," he said rising, and looking at Billy so hard that it made his cheeks feel hot, "why, Bradford, I didn't know that you had a son."

"I haven't a son, sir," said John Bradford. "This is my nephew, William Wallace Bradford."

Billy's cheeks cooled off very fast, and his heart seemed to move down in his side; for it was the very first time that Uncle John had ever called him by his whole name.

"You couldn't deny that he belongs to you, even if you wanted to," said the superintendent, "for his eyes are a real Bradford blue. Anything like you except his eyes?" he added quizzically.

"I'm glad that he belongs to me, Mr. Prescott," answered John Bradford, putting his hand on Billy's shoulder. "He's a good boy, too. Can't say just what I was, when I was thirteen."

"There's some difference between a boy and a man, I'll admit," said the superintendent; "but what I'm driving at is that I need an office boy, this very minute, and I should like a Bradford boy. What do you say, Bradford?"

"Eh, Billy, my lad?" said Uncle John.

Even in the moment that they had been standing there, something in the tall, broad-shouldered man, who looked earnestly down at him, had touched Billy's hero-spring. As soon as he heard the question, he knew that he wanted to be Mr. Prescott's office boy. So, forgetting all about his birthday and everything else, he said, with his William Wallace promptness, "I'll begin right away, sir."

"Well then, William," said the superintendent, in his firm, business tone, "as my office boy, you must keep your eyes and your ears open, and your lips shut. Understand?"

Then, before Billy could answer, Mr. Prescott gave him a letter, saying, "Post that on the train."

Billy darted through the door, and the superintendent sat down at his desk.

"Thank you, sir," said John Bradford; and, just then, the whistle blew.

Billy did more errands that afternoon than he had ever done in a whole day; several times he had to put on extra whistle power to keep his legs going. But he was proud and happy that night when they told Aunt Mary the news. He saw the look of relief that came into her face; and, though that made him glad, it made him a little sorry, too.

After supper he went out in the path to look once more at the mountains growing dim and blue in the summer twilight. He knew, now, what he had not known in the morning; and that was, how he was going to help to take care of himself.

He stood there until his aunt called, "William Wallace, it's time to come in."

Then his wish of the morning—the wish of his heart— asserted itself once more; and, as he turned to go into the house, he said, half in a whisper:

"I wisht she'd call me Billy."

CHAPTER II

OLD IRON

AYS don't always come out as we expect they will," said Uncle John, as he and Billy started out together the next morning. "But it's your birthday, just the same. Shut your eyes and hold out your hand. Ready."

Billy, opening his eyes, saw his uncle holding a jack-knife, which dangled from a chain.

"Just what I wanted," exclaimed Billy, taking the knife.

"Thought it would be handy for an office boy," said Uncle John, beaming with satisfaction. "I'm going," said he, as Billy put his dinner pail down on the sidewalk and opened both blades, "to give you something else, something to carry around in your head, instead of in your pocket. It's an office boy motto: Whatever you do, do it right, just as right as you can."

"That isn't any new news," said Billy, looking rather disappointed. "You told me that a long time ago."

"Come to think of it, I did," said Uncle John. "It's good for any boy, any time; but it's specially good for an office boy. I should like to talk it over, but we shall have to hurry now."

7

Together they went through the gate, and stood in line, while lame Tom, the timekeeper, made marks against their names. Then Uncle John said cheerily, "Meet me behind the mill when the noon whistle blows."

"Sure, sir," said Billy.

Billy went on, through the great door, down the narrow corridor, and had a "good-morning" all ready to say when he opened the office door.

Of course, he didn't find anybody there. The office didn't seem to be in very good order; but nobody had told him what he was expected to do.

So he looked around for a moment. Then he put his pail on a stool in the corner, and picked up a pencil that lay on the floor under Mr. Prescott's desk. The point was broken. That made him think of his knife. Then he looked for a waste-basket, for Aunt Mary was very particular about not having shavings and lead on the floor. On the top of the waste-basket he found a duster. Billy knew a duster when he saw it, for dusting was one of the things that Aunt Mary had taught him to do.

When the pencil was done—it was very well done, for he used both blades of his knife to do it—he put it on top of Mr. Prescott's desk, and began to dust in good earnest.

When the postman came in, he looked a little surprised, but all he said was:

"New boy, are you?"

"Yes, sir," answered Billy.

Then he put the letters in one pile and the papers in another, and was putting a finishing touch with his duster on the rungs of Mr. Prescott's chair when he came in.

Billy was so busy that he didn't hear him till he said, "Good-morning, William."

"Good-morning, sir. Where shall I empty the waste-basket?"

"Really," said Mr. Prescott, "unexpected pleasure, I am sure—barrel outside."

Billy had hoped that Mr. Prescott would notice how well he had sharpened the pencil; but he put it into his pocket without saying a word.

Perhaps he did see more than he seemed to, for, when the expressman came in with a package, Mr. Prescott said, "William, cut the string."

When Billy took out his knife, Mr. Prescott glanced up from his papers, saying, "Unexpected pleasure, really."

Billy was beginning to feel that being an office boy wasn't a bit social, when Mr. Prescott said:

"William, why is a jack-knife called a jack-knife?"

"I don't know, sir."

"Frenchman named Jacques first made them," said Mr. Prescott.

Billy wanted very much to tell him where his knife came from; but he didn't feel sure that office boys were supposed to have birthdays.

Then the stenographer came; and, before Billy knew it, it was noon, and he went to meet Uncle John behind the mill.

"Birthday coming on pretty well, Billy?" asked Uncle John, as they both opened their pails.

"Sure," answered Billy, who was so hungry that he couldn't stop to talk.

"Sorry we couldn't celebrate," said Uncle John. "Mustn't

give up the idea though, Billy. As you go around on errands, you'll see a good many things. Some day we'll piece them together. Watch for a chance and it'll come some day."

Billy, fast nearing the bottom of his pail, paused a moment to say, "Uncle John, were you ever an office boy?"

"Not just that," answered Uncle John.

"There's a lot to it," said Billy.

"I suppose there is," said Uncle John, gravely. "There is to almost anything, if you do it right."

After that, Billy's days went on, one very like another. It seemed to him that there was no end to the things he had to learn. He had very little time to spend in wishing, though every night he went out for a good look at the mountains. But he was beginning to think about the kind of man that he would like to be; and every day he was a little more sure that he wanted to be like the young superintendent.

He was so short himself that he was afraid that he would never be as tall as Mr. Prescott. So he began to stand as tall as he could, especially when he was in the office. Then he tried to remember to breathe deep, the way that the teacher at school had told the boys to do. But he wondered, sometimes, when he looked at Mr. Prescott's broad shoulders, whether he had ever been as small as most boys.

The day that Billy had his first little brown envelope with three dollars and fifty cents in it, he stood very tall indeed. That night, at supper, he handed it to Aunt Mary, saying:

"That's for you to put in the bank."

"For Billy," said Uncle John, looking up quickly and speaking almost sternly. "I'm the one to give Aunt Mary money."

Then he said gently: "It's a good plan, Billy, to put your first money in the bank. You'll never have any more just like that."

The thing that first excited Billy's curiosity, as he went about on errands, was the big pile of old iron in the mill yard. There were pieces of old stoves, and seats from schoolhouses that had been burned, and engines that had been smashed in wrecks, and old ploughs, and nobody knew what else—all piled up in a great heap.

One day, when he carried an order to the man that tended the furnace in the cupola where they melted the iron, he saw them putting pieces of old iron on the scales; and he heard the man say to his helper: "We shall have to put in fifty pounds extra to-day."

It seemed to Billy that it wasn't quite fair to put in old iron, when they were making new machinery. So, one noon, he asked Uncle John about it.

"Using your eyes, are you, Billy? That's quite likely to set your mind to working.

"I suppose you've heard them talking around here about testing machinery. That isn't the first testing. They test iron all the way along, from the ore in the mine to the sticks of pig iron piled up in our yard."

"Some of it is in cakes," said Billy.

"Is that so?" asked Uncle John, as he took another sandwich out of his pail. "Now I think of it, they did tell me that cakes are the new style in pig iron.

"Well," continued Uncle John, "there are men testing and experimenting all the time; and some of them found out that old iron and pig iron together make better new iron than they can make from pig iron alone. Since they found that out, scrap iron has kept on going up in price.

"Did you happen, Billy, to see any other heaps lying around?"

"I saw a pile of coke, over in the corner," answered Billy.

"Somewhere," said Uncle John, "there must have been a heap of limestone. They use that for what they call a flux. That unites with the waste things, the ashes of the coke and any sand that may have stuck to the pig iron. Those things together make slag. The slag is so much lighter than the iron that it floats on top, and there are tap holes in the cupola where they draw it off. Limestone helps the iron to melt, that's another reason why they use it."

"I saw some scales," said Billy.

"Those," said Uncle John, "are to weigh the things that they put into the cupola. There are rules for making cast iron. It all depends on what kind of machinery we want to make.

"First, in the bottom of the cupola, they make a fire of shavings and wood, with a little coal; then they put in coke, pig iron, scrap iron, and limestone, according to the rule for the kind of iron that they want to make.

"Those heaps all pieced together, Billy."

"Sure," answered Billy; and, then, the whistle blew.

Deep down in his heart, Billy didn't like that whistle. He didn't tell Uncle John, because William Wallace scorned anybody who felt like that. William Wallace said that being on time—on time to the minute—was only just business. Nevertheless, Billy missed being free. Aunt Mary's errands hadn't been timed by the clock.

There was another reason why he didn't tell Uncle John how he felt.

"Stand by your job, every minute that you belong on it," was one of the things that Uncle John had said so many times that it almost worried Billy.

But, before the summer was over, Billy was glad that he had kept that on his mind.

CHAPTER III

A MOUNTAIN OF IRON

HETHER, if it hadn't been for Billy's new jack-knife, he and Thomas Murphy would have become friends, no one can say. It seems very probable that something would have made them like each other.

Sitting on a high stool to check time or in a chair to watch the great door had grown so monotonous that Tom really needed to have somebody to talk to.

Then there wasn't any boy in the mill for Billy to get acquainted with; and Billy saw Tom oftener than he saw any of the other men. So it seems very natural that Billy and Tom should have become friends.

If they hadn't, things wouldn't have turned out just as they did; and whatever else might have happened, it was really the jack-knife that brought them together.

Billy had been in the mill about two weeks when, one morning, just as Tom was finishing making a mark after Uncle John's name, snap went the point of his pencil.

Billy heard it break, and saw Tom put his hand into his

14

pocket. Billy knew, from Tom's face, before he drew his hand out, that there wasn't any knife in his pocket.

So Billy put his dinner pail down, and pulling his knife out by the chain, said quickly:

"I'll sharpen your pencil, Mr. Murphy."

Billy had been practicing on sharpening pencils. He worked so fast that the men behind had hardly begun to grumble before the pencil was in working order, and the line began to move on again.

Though he did not know it, Billy had done something more than merely to sharpen Tom's pencil. When he said, "Mr. Murphy," he waked up something in Tom that Tom himself had almost forgotten about.

He had been called "Tom Murphy" so long, sometimes only "lame Tom," that Billy's saying "Mr. Murphy" had made him sit up very straight, while he was waiting for Billy to sharpen the pencil.

Mr. Prescott thought that he really appreciated Tom. He always said, "Tom Murphy is as faithful as the day is long"; but even Mr. Prescott didn't know so much about Tom as he thought he did. If Billy and Tom hadn't become friends, Mr. Prescott would probably never have learned anything about the "Mr. Murphy" side of Tom.

After that morning, Billy and Tom kept on getting acquainted, until one day when Uncle John had to go out one noon to see about some new window screens for Aunt Mary, Billy went to the door to see Tom.

Tom, having just sat down in his chair, was trying to get his lame leg into a position where it would be more comfortable.

"Does your leg hurt, Mr. Murphy?" asked Billy.

"Pretty bad to-day, William," answered Thomas Murphy with a groan. "If it wasn't so dry, I should think, from the way my leg aches, that it was going to rain, but there's no hope of that."

"It's rheumatism, isn't it?" asked Billy, sympathetically.

"Part of it is," answered Tom, "but before that it was crush. I hope you don't think I've never done anything but mark time at Prescott mill. I suppose that you think you've seen considerable iron in this yard and in this mill; but you don't know half so much about iron as I did when my legs were as good as yours.

"Out West, where I was born, there are acres and acres and acres of iron almost on top of the ground; and, besides that, a whole mountain of iron."

Tom paused a moment to move his leg again.

"Was there an iron mine in the ground, too?" asked Billy, sitting down on the threshold of the door.

"Yes, there was," answered Tom. "If I had stayed on top of the ground, perhaps I shouldn't have been hurt. Might have been blown up in a gopher hole, though, the way my brother was."

"O-oh!" said Billy.

"Never heard of a gopher hole, I suppose," continued Tom, settling back in his chair, as though he intended to improve his opportunity to talk.

"That's one way that they get iron out of a mountain. They make holes straight into a bank. Then they put in sacks of powder, and fire it with a fuse. That loosens the ore so that they can use a steam shovel. Sometimes the men go in too soon."

"I wish," said Billy with a little shiver, "that you would tell me about the mine."

"That'll be quite a contract," said Thomas Murphy, clasping his hands across his chest, "but I was in one long enough to know.

"You'll think there was a mine down in the ground when I tell you that I've been down a thousand feet in one myself. I went down that one in a cage; but in the mine where I worked I used to go down on ladders at the side of the shaft."

"Was it something like a coal mine?" asked Billy.

"I've heard miners say," answered Tom, "that some iron is so hard that it has to be worked with a pick and a shovel; but the iron in our mine was so soft that we caved it down. If I had been working with a pick, perhaps I shouldn't have been hurt.

"When you cave iron, you go down to the bottom of the shaft and work under the iron. You cut out a place, and put in some big timbers to hold up the roof. Then you cut some more, and keep on till you think the roof may fall.

"Then you board that place in, and knock out some pillars, or blow them out, and down comes the iron. Then you put it in a car and push it to a chute, and that loads it on an elevator to be brought up. Sometimes they use electric trams; we used to have to push the cars."

"It must be very hard work," said Billy.

"Work, William, usually is hard," said Thomas Murphy. "Work, underground or above ground, is work, William."

"But you haven't told me, Mr. Murphy," said Billy, "how you hurt your knee."

"The quickest way to tell you that, William, is to tell you that the cave, that time, caved too soon. I got caught on the edge of it.

"After I got out of the hospital, I tried to work above ground; but the noise of the steam shovels and the blasting wore me out.

So, one day, I took an ore train, and went to the boat and came up the river. Finally, I drifted to Prescott mill, some seasons before you were born, William."

"Have you ever wanted to go back?" asked Billy.

"No, William, I haven't. There's nobody left out there that belongs to me, anyway. My lame knee wasn't the only reason why I left, William. I heard something about the country that I didn't like at all; I didn't like it at all."

"Weren't the people good?" asked Billy.

"Very good people," answered Thomas Murphy firmly. "'Twas something about the mountain that I heard.

"There were always men around examining the mines. I never paid much attention to 'em till one day I heard a man—they said he came from some college—a-talking about volcanoes. He said that iron mountain was thrown up by a volcano, said he was sure of it.

"I never told anybody, William, but I cleared out the very next day. You've never heard anything about volcanoes round here, have you, William?"

"No, Mr. Murphy," answered Billy.

"If you ever should, William," said Thomas Murphy, leaning anxiously forward.

"If I ever do hear, Mr. Murphy," said Billy, feeling that he was making a promise, "I'll tell you right away."

"Thank you, William," said Tom. "You won't mention it, will you?"

"No, Mr. Murphy," answered Billy.

That was really the day when Billy and Thomas Murphy sealed their compact as friends.

CHAPTER IV

THE FOUNDRY

Y friend, Mr. Murphy," said Billy, one night after supper, when he and Uncle John were sitting side by side on the steps.

"Did I understand?" interrupted Uncle John, "Mr. Murphy?"

"Yes," answered Billy, "Mr. Thomas Murphy the timekeeper."

"Exactly," said Uncle John.

"Mr. Murphy," Billy went on, "says that iron moves the world."

"I should say," said Uncle John, deliberately, "that power generally has to be put into an iron harness before anything can move; but Mr. Murphy evidently knows what he is talking about."

"He says," continued Billy, "that iron mills are very important places; and that, for his part, he's glad that he works in an iron mill."

"That's the way every man ought to feel about his work," said Uncle John; "all the work in the world has to be done by somebody."

19

That remark sounded to Billy as if another motto might be coming; and, being tired, he wanted just to be social. So he said: "Uncle John, did you ever see Miss King, the stenographer?"

"Only coming and going," he answered.

"She's a friend of mine, too," said Billy. "She told me, to-day, that she wants me always to feel that she is my friend."

"Everything going all right in the office, Billy?" asked Uncle John, quickly.

"Oh, yes," answered Billy, with a little note of happiness in his voice. "She told me that so as to make me feel comfortable. She's the loveliest woman I ever saw. Don't you think, Uncle John, that yellow-brown is the prettiest color for hair?"

"I do," said Uncle John, emphatically. Then, rising to go into the house, he added, "That's exactly what I used to call Aunt Mary's hair, yellow-brown."

"Oh!" said Billy wonderingly. Then it was time for him to go to bed; but he lingered a moment to look at Aunt Mary's hair that was dark brown, now, where it wasn't gray. There was something in his "Good-night, Aunt Mary," that made her look up from her paper as she said:

"Good-night, William Wallace."

Anybody can see that William Wallace is a hard name for a boy to go to bed on. It was so hard for Billy that it almost hurt; but Billy had lived with Aunt Mary long enough to be sure that she meant to be a true friend.

Whether or not Mr. Prescott was his friend, Billy did not know. Mr. Murphy had told him one day when he was out by the door, waiting for the postman, that Mr. Prescott was a friend to every man in the mill. Billy supposed that every man was a friend back again. At any rate, he knew that he was; and he hoped that, some day, he would be able to do something, just to show Mr. Prescott how much he liked him.

The more he thought about it, the more it didn't seem possible that such a hope as that could ever come true.

But anybody who liked anybody else as much as he liked Mr. Prescott couldn't help seeing that something bothered him. So Billy had a little secret with himself to try to look specially pleasant when Mr. Prescott came in from a trip around the mill. He had begun to think that Mr. Prescott had given up springing questions on him when, one very warm afternoon, Mr. Prescott looked up from his desk and said:

"William, if you were to have an afternoon off, what would you do?"

"I'd rather than anything else in the world," answered Billy promptly, "go out into the country."

"That being hardly feasible," said Mr. Prescott, "what else would you rather do?"

"Next to that," answered Billy, "I'd rather go into the foundry to see Uncle John work."

"Well!" exclaimed Mr. Prescott, whirling around in his chair. "That's about the last thing that I should have thought of, especially on such a hot day. May I inquire whether you are interested in iron?"

Billy, with a quick flash of spirit, answered promptly, "I am, sir."

As promptly Mr. Prescott said, "I'm glad to hear it, William. You may spend the rest of the afternoon in the foundry."

"Thank you, sir," said Billy, very much surprised. Then he looked at Miss King, and she nodded and smiled.

Billy ran down the corridor, passing Mr. Murphy with a flying salute, and hurried across the yard to the foundry door.

Just then he remembered that he hadn't a permit; but the foreman appeared in the door saying, "The super has telephoned over that you're to visit us this afternoon."

Pointing across the room, he added, "Your uncle is over there."

Billy wanted to surprise his Uncle John, so he went carefully along the outer side of the long, low room, past pile after pile of gray black sand, until he came to the place where Uncle John was bending over what seemed to be a long bar of sand.

"Uncle John," he said softly.

"Why, Billy, my lad!" exclaimed he, looking up with so much surprise in his face that Billy said quickly:

"It's all right, Uncle John. Mr. Prescott sent me to watch you work."

"Things," said Uncle John, with a smile that made wrinkles around his eyes, "generally come round right if you wait for them."

"What is that?" asked Billy, pointing at the bar.

"That is a mold for a lathe," answered Uncle John. "I'm nearly through with it, then I'm going to help out on corn cutters. We have a rush order on corn canning machines. You'd better sit on that box till I'm through."

Billy looked at the tiny trowel in Uncle John's hand, and saw him take off a little sand in one place, and put some on in another, until the mold was smooth and even. Then he tested his corners with what he called a "corner slick."

"I never supposed that you worked that way," said Billy, "but Miss King told me that molders are artists in sand."

"Did she, though?" said Uncle John, straightening up to take a final look at his work. "I'll remember that.

"Now we'll go over where they are working on the corn cutters. It's a little cooler on that side."

"Where does black sand come from?" asked Billy.

"It's yellow," answered his uncle, "when we begin to use it, but the action of the hot iron, as we use it, over and over, turns it black."

Then came the work that Billy had waited so long to see.

Uncle John took a wooden frame—he called it a drag—which was about two feet square and not quite so deep. He put it on a bench high enough for him to work easily. Then he laid six cutters for a corn canning machine, side by side, in the bottom of the box.

"Those," he said, "are patterns."

Taking a sieve—a riddle—he filled it with moist sand which he sifted over the cutters. Next, with his fingers, he packed the sand carefully around the patterns. Then, with a shovel, he filled the drag with sand, and rammed it down with a wooden rammer until the drag was full.

"Now," said he, taking up a wire, "I am going to make some vent holes, so the steam can escape."

When that was done, he clamped a top on the box, turned it over, and took out the bottom.

Billy could see the cutters, bedded firm in the sand.

Blowing off the loose sand with bellows, and smoothing the sand around the pattern, Uncle John took some dry sand, which he sifted through his fingers, blowing it off where it touched the cutters.

"This sand," he said, "will keep the two parts of the mold

He Filled it with Moist Sand

from sticking together." Then he took another frame, a cope, which was like the first, except that it had pins on the sides, where the other had sockets. Slipping the pins into the sockets, he fastened them together.

Taking two round, tapering plugs of wood, he set them firmly in the sand, at each end of the patterns.

"One of those," said he, "will make a place for the hot iron to go in, and the other for it to rise up on the other side."

Then he filled the second box as he had the first, and made more vent holes.

"Billy," he said, suddenly, "where are those corn cutters?"

"In the middle of the box," answered Billy promptly, just as if he had always known about molding in sand.

"Now," said Uncle John, "comes the artist part."

Lifting the second part off the first, he turned it over carefully and set it on the bench.

"There they are," exclaimed Billy.

"There they are," said Uncle John, with a smile, "but there they are not going to remain."

Dipping a sponge in water, he wet the sand around the edges of the pattern. Then he screwed a draw spike into the middle of the pattern and rapped it gently with a mallet to loosen it from the sand.

"Pretty nearly perfect, aren't they?" he said, when he had them all safely out. "Now for some real artist work."

With a lifter he took out the sand that had fallen into the mold, patched a tiny break here and there, and tested the corners.

Last of all he made grooves, which he called "gates," between the patterns, and also at the ends where the iron was to be poured in.

Then he clamped the two boxes together. "Now the holes are in the middle," said he, "and I hope that they will stay there till the iron is poured in."

Billy, sitting on a box, watched Uncle John till he had finished another set of molds.

"That all clear so far?" asked Uncle John.

"Sure," answered Billy.

"Think you could do it yourself?" broke in a heavy voice.

Billy, looking up, saw the foreman, who had been watching Billy while he watched his uncle.

"I think I know how," answered Billy.

"If you won't talk to the men," said the foreman, "you may walk around the foundry until we are ready to pour."

So Billy walked slowly around the long foundry. He saw that each man had his own pile of sand, but the piles were growing very small, because the day's work was nearly over. The molds were being put in rows for the pouring.

He had walked nearly back to his Uncle John when he happened to step in a hollow place in the earth floor and, losing his balance, fell against a man who was carrying a mold.

With a strange, half-muttered expression the man pushed his elbow against Billy and almost threw him down.

Billy, looking up into a pair of fierce black eyes that glared at him from under a mass of coal black hair, turned so pale that William Wallace then and there called him a coward.

As fast as his feet would carry him Billy went back to Uncle John, who, still busy with his molds, said:

"Go out behind the foundry and look in at the window to see us pour."

Billy, for the first time in his life thoroughly frightened, was glad to go out into the open air.

Then he went to the window opposite the great cupola to wait for the pouring.

There at the left of the furnace door stood the foundry foreman, tall and strong, holding a long iron rod in his hand. He, too, was waiting.

Then, because Billy had thought and thought over what Uncle John had told him about pouring, his mind began to make a picture; and when sparks of fire from the spout shot across the foundry, the cupola became a fiery dragon and the foreman a noble knight, bearing a long iron spear.

Only once breathed the dragon; for the knight, heedless of danger, closed the iron mouth with a single thrust of his spear.

Another wait. This time the knight forced the dragon to open his mouth, and the yielding dragon sent out his pointed, golden tongue.

But only for a moment; for again the knight thrust in his iron spear.

At last the knight gave way to the dragon.

Then, wonder of wonders, from the dragon's mouth there came a golden, molten stream.

When the great iron ladle below was almost filled, the knight closed once more the dragon's mouth.

Two by two came men bearing between them long-handled iron ladles. The great ladle swung forward, for a moment, on its tilting gear, and the men bore away their ladles filled with iron that the great dragon had changed from its own dull gray to the brilliant yellow of gold.

The molds, as they were filled, smoked from all their

venting places, till, to his picture, Billy added a place for a battle-field.

By the time that the last molds were filled, some of the men began to take off the wooden frames, and there the iron was, gray again, but, this time, shaped for the use of man.

"See," said Uncle John, coming to the window, "there are our corn cutters. Came out pretty well, didn't they?"

"Wasn't it great!" exclaimed Billy.

"Just about as wonderful every time," said Uncle John.

"What do they do next?" asked Billy.

"Make new heaps of sand—every man his own heap—and in the morning, after the castings have been carried into the mill, they begin all over again."

"I'm so glad I saw it," said Billy, drawing a deep breath of satisfaction.

That night he told Aunt Mary about what he had seen. And he thought about it almost until he fell asleep. Almost, but not quite; for, just as he was dozing off, William Wallace said:

"You were frightened—frightened. You showed a white feather!"

Half asleep as he was, Billy, tired of William Wallace's superior airs, roused himself long enough to say: "We'll see who has white feathers."

CHAPTER V

THE GREAT IRON KEY

ULY was hot. Everybody said so. The sun burned the grass in the yards till it was brown, and no rain came to make it green again. All the men were tired; some of them were cross.

Mr. Prescott put in more electric fans. Then he played the hose to keep the air cool, but the water supply was so low that he was ordered to stop using the hose.

One day he had an awning put up near the gate, and sent lame Tom Murphy, the timekeeper, out there to sit.

Tom, preferring the cool of the great door where he had always sat, confided his trouble to Billy.

"It's my opinion," he said, "privately spoken to you alone, that the super sent me out here for something besides air. It's been my opinion, for some time, that there's trouble somewhere."

"I suppose," said Billy, assuming a business tone, "that you're a friend back again, aren't you, Mr. Murphy?"

29

Unconsciously sitting straighter in his chair, he answered, "I'm not altogether clear as to your meaning, William."

"You told me yourself, Mr. Murphy," said Billy, still speaking very firmly, "that Mr. Prescott is a friend to every man in the mill. Aren't you a friend back again?"

"I am," answered the timekeeper emphatically. "You may depend on me in all weathers, even to sitting out here in the sun."

"Then," said Billy, "you and I, Mr. Murphy, are both friends, on our honor as gentlemen—that's what my father used to say."

"I am," answered Thomas Murphy.

Just then they heard the honk, honk of Mr. Prescott's machine, and Billy stood carefully aside for him to pass.

Mr. Prescott, who was alone, said:

"Things all right, Thomas? Jump in, William."

Billy, surprised beyond words, obeyed.

Mr. Prescott, starting the car quickly, drove rapidly down the street.

When they reached the square, Billy said:

"Some letters, sir, to post. That's where I was going."

"Very well," said Mr. Prescott, stopping the car.

"Ever in a machine before?" he asked, as Billy got in again beside him.

"No, sir."

"Think I'll take you with me then; I'm chasing an order. We're nearly out of coke."

They rode so fast that the air began to seem cooler. Billy, quite willing to be silent with Mr. Prescott beside him, settled back in the seat in blissful content.

"Know anything about coke, William?" asked Mr. Prescott, breaking the silence, suddenly.

"No, sir, except that it's gray, and that they burn it in the cupola."

"Oh, yes, I remember," said Mr. Prescott; "you're interested in iron. Well, then, it's time that you knew something about coke.

"Long ago they used charcoal, that is, partly burned wood, in the iron furnaces. That used up the forests so fast that, over in England, the government had to limit the number of iron furnaces.

"Then they tried to use coal. That didn't work very well. Finally, somebody found that, if the coal was partly burned, that is, made into coke, it would require less blast, and the iron would melt more quickly. It was a great day for iron when coke came in."

The car sped on, and again Mr. Prescott lapsed into silence.

The country didn't look at all like the country that Billy dreamed about. His was green. This was brown. But there were no hot, red bricks to look at; that was something to be thankful for, anyway.

"See anything new?" asked Mr. Prescott.

"What are they?" asked Billy, pointing to long rows of something that looked like large beehives.

"Coke ovens; they call them beehive ovens. That overhead railway is where they charge the ovens through the top. After the coal has burned about two days, it is quenched with water. Then they draw it out at the bottom as coke, and put in a new charge while the ovens are still hot."

After he got home that night—it was closing time when

they reached the square where Mr. Prescott left him—Billy couldn't remember that Mr. Prescott had said a word to him all the way back. But Billy was happy, and rested, too.

While they were walking to the mill the next morning Uncle John said:

"Billy, my lad, I want to give you some confidential advice. You went out riding with the superintendent yesterday, didn't you?"

"Yes, sir," answered Billy.

"But you're the office boy, just the same, this morning?"

"Sure, Uncle John," answered Billy.

"I thought you'd be clear on that," said Uncle John, beaming with pride. "I thought you'd be clear on that!"

Billy began the day as an office boy, dusting and sharpening pencils and sorting the mail. Miss King came in, looking cool and pretty in her white office dress, with a bunch of sweet peas in her hand.

"Beautiful, aren't they, William?" she said holding them up in the light. "See how the lavender ones have pink in them, and the pink have white, and the white are just tinted with pink, so they all blend together. I always pick some leaves, too; they're such a soft, cool green."

"Do you suppose," asked Billy, "that they'd grow in a yard—just a common yard?"

"These grew in our backyard," answered Miss King. "I'll give you some seed next year."

At that moment Mr. Prescott came in with a telegram in his hand.

"Have to catch the nine-forty express," he said. "Can't get back for three days, anyway. Open those letters, William."

Out came Billy's knife, and he opened letters while Mr. Prescott dictated to Miss King.

"Don't," said Mr. Prescott, seizing his hat, "let anybody know that I have gone if you can help it. Don't tell them how long I shall be gone. You and William must look after everything."

Then off he went, leaving Miss King and Billy looking at each other in dismay.

"Well," said Miss King, after a moment, "we don't know where he has gone. So we can't tell anybody that. And we don't know when he is coming back. It isn't very likely," she added, with a reassuring smile, "that anything will happen while he is gone."

Billy, who had never forgotten about keeping his ears open, thought Miss King said "very" as if she weren't quite sure about something. So he said:

"I'll stay in here with you as much as I can."

"Thank you," said Miss King, smiling. "There's nothing to do, anyway," she went on, half to herself, "except to do things as they come along. So we'll do that, William. Please get me some water for the flowers."

Then she opened the typewriter and began to write very fast.

The day went on very much like other days. The mill seemed almost to be running itself. When they were leaving the office that night Miss King said cheerfully:

"We've had a very pleasant day, haven't we, William?"

"Seems to me I haven't worked so hard as usual," answered Billy.

The next day when Billy came back from the bank, soon

after the noon whistle had blown, lame Tom's chair under the canopy by the gate was empty.

Billy, hurrying on to the main building, found that Tom's chair by the great door was empty, too.

As he stepped inside, Tom appeared from behind the door.

When he saw Billy an expression of relief came into his face.

"I'm glad to see you, William," he said. "Stand in the door a minute and pretend I'm not talking to you."

Billy, wondering what could have happened, turned his back on Tom, and waited.

"William," said Tom, in an almost sepulchral tone, "the great key is gone."

Billy nearly jumped out the door. But, remembering that he was on duty to look after things, he said:

"You watch while I try to find it."

Even Billy's young eyes could not find the key. He searched till he was sure, then he said:

"I'll look again, Mr. Murphy, after you go out to the gate."

The key was one of Mr. Prescott's special treasures, for it was the very one that his grandfather had when he first built the mill. Several times the door had been almost made over, but the key had never been changed.

It was an iron key—three times as long as Billy's longest finger, with a bow in which three of his fingers and almost a fourth could lie side by side, and its bit was more than half as long as his thumb. It was so large that Mr. Prescott sometimes called lame Tom "the keeper of the great key."

Gone it was. Billy hunted till he was sure of that. He wanted to tell Miss King about it, but he could not stop to tell her then, for he had to distribute the orders for the afternoon.

Here and there he went. Last of all he had to go into the foundry. He was halfway down the room before he realized that he was on the side where he must pass the man with the fierce eyes and the coal black hair. Determined this time to be brave, he went steadily on.

The man was standing still, bending over his drag, his shock of unkempt hair hanging down over his eyes. He was so intent on his work that Billy, so nearly past that he felt quite safe, looked down curiously to see what pattern the man was using.

There, all by itself, in the bottom of the box, lay the great iron key.

CHAPTER VI

A SURPRISE OR TWO

HE sight of the key did something more than to make Billy's eyes open very wide; it struck to his legs. They grew so heavy that, for a minute, he couldn't lift them at all. But he kept on trying, and finally succeeded in pulling up first one, and then the other, and in starting them both. Then they wanted to move fast, and he had hard work to slow them down to simply a quick walk. At last he reached the door, and hurried across the yard and down the corridor to the office.

When he opened the door, something struck to his feet, and fairly glued them to the threshold.

There at his desk, writing away hard, sat Mr. Prescott.

Billy's blue eyes, large from seeing the key, grew still larger, so that, when Mr. Prescott finally looked up, he saw quite a different boy from the Billy whom he had left only the day before.

"Well, William," he said, as he put down his pen, "having obeyed to the letter—I might say to the period—my injunction to keep your lips shut, suppose you open them."

36

Billy's tongue seemed to be fastened to the roof of his mouth tighter than his feet were to the floor, and he couldn't seem to unfasten it.

"Perhaps," continued Mr. Prescott, "it might be as well, just at this point, for me to inform you that surprise is one of the persistent elements of business. I met another telegram, so you meet me. What has happened?"

When Billy finally reached the desk and began to tell him about the key, Mr. Prescott whirled around in his chair and put his right thumb into the right armhole of his vest.

Before Billy had finished, though his tongue, having started, went very fast, Mr. Prescott put his other thumb in his other armhole, and leaned back in his chair till his shoulders seemed almost to fill the space between the desk and the railing.

"Well," he said, when Billy had finished, "as you are the one in possession of the original facts, what do you think had better be done?"

If Mr. Prescott had only known it, Billy didn't like him very well when he talked that way. But of course nobody can like anybody every minute of the time; for even a best hero is more than likely to have disagreeable spots. Billy's father had told him that, and Billy was very much like his father in the way he had of forgetting disagreeables pretty soon after they happened. Just that minute, anyway, his whole mind was on that great iron key.

Besides, when Mr. Prescott talked that way, he always hit the man-side of Billy. Possibly Mr. Prescott knew that.

"I think, sir," answered Billy, almost before he knew what he was saying, "that I can get the key."

"Oh, you do, do you?" said Mr. Prescott. "Will you be so kind as to tell me about what time today you will deliver it?"

Billy looked at the clock.

Miss King's keys kept right on—clickety-clickety-click.

Billy changed his weight to his other foot before he answered:

"About four o'clock, sir."

Mr. Prescott looked at the clock, then he took up his pen, saying:

"It is now nearly half-past three. It would be a pity, in such an important matter, for you to fail for lack of time to work out any little theory that you happen to have originated. Suppose we make it half-past four o'clock."

As Billy started for the door Mr. Prescott added:

"Having opened your lips, you may close them again, a little tighter than before. Understand?"

"Yes, sir," answered Billy.

"Mind," called Mr. Prescott, when Billy had almost closed the door, "you are to return at half-past four, key or no key."

"Sure, sir," answered Billy.

Things don't always look the same on both sides of a door. Billy found that out as soon as he was alone in the corridor. But Billy had a theory, though Mr. Prescott may have thought that he was joking, and it was built on so firm a foundation that William Wallace offered, at once, to help him work it out.

Billy hadn't visited Uncle John that day in the foundry simply for nothing. He had it all figured out in his mind that, as soon as the black-haired man had finished using the key for a pattern, he would put it back in the door; and Billy had said four o'clock because that was about the time when the molds were supposed to be ready.

When a man knew as much about molding as Mr. Prescott did, it did seem as if he might have figured that out himself.

Billy looked around for a place where he could hide to watch the door. There wasn't anybody in sight, so he took plenty of time to decide.

Half-way down the corridor, on the right-hand side, was a small closet that had been built up on the floor, by itself, so that Mr. Prescott could have a place to keep his motor clothes.

Billy went into that, and tried, by leaving the door partway open, to fix a crack through which he could watch the door. Finding that the crack was too far out of range, he started down the corridor to find another place.

He had just about decided to try hiding behind the tool room when he heard a step, and, looking up, saw Thomas Murphy, the timekeeper.

"It's a great relief, William," said Tom, "to see a friend like you. Does the super know about the key?"

Billy looked at Tom, and Tom looked at Billy. Bad as Tom felt, Billy felt three times worse. Billy had three things on his mind: first of all, he mustn't tell a lie; then, he must keep the secret; and, if Tom Murphy stayed by that door, the man wouldn't bring back the key.

Billy and William Wallace both thought as fast as they could. Billy got hold of an idea first. Perhaps by asking Tom a question he could throw him off the track, and could keep from telling a lie. So he said: "Had you made up your mind, Mr. Murphy, when it would be best to tell him?"

"No, William," answered Tom Murphy, in a hopeless tone,

"I hadn't. I've turned that thing over and over in my mind, and I've turned it inside out; and all the answer that I can get to it is that there'll be no Tom Murphy any more a-keepin' time at Prescott mill."

"But you didn't lose the key, Mr. Murphy," said Billy, very sympathetically, now that his first danger was over.

"That I didn't," said Tom Murphy. "It's been a rule and a regulation that that key was to stay in that door from morning to night. That key ought not to have been left in that door."

"No," said Billy, "excepting that everybody knows how much Mr. Prescott thinks of that key."

"That's just it," said Thomas Murphy, pulling his old chair out from behind the door, and sinking into it with a sigh of relief.

"What would you," he asked as he stretched out his lame leg, and clasped his hands across his chest, "what would you advise, as a friend? Don't leave me, William," he exclaimed, as Billy stepped outside.

"I won't," said Billy, stepping forward far enough to see the clock.

Fifteen minutes gone! Where had fifteen minutes gone?

"Do you think, William," asked Thomas Murphy, as Billy went back to him, "that, if the super never finds that key, there will be any Thomas Murphy any more a-keepin' time at Prescott mill?"

"You know," said Billy, "that Mr. Prescott is a friend to everybody. I think," he added slowly, because he was trying to keep still and at the same time to be wise, "I think he would be—more of—a friend—to a man—than to a key."

"His grandfather's key?" said Tom solemnly.

"His grandfather's key," repeated Billy, backing toward the door, and stepping out.

Five minutes of four!

Looking over at the foundry, Billy saw a man with shaggy black hair who, with his right hand pressed close against his side, was stepping back into the foundry door!

Billy himself stepped quickly back.

"William," said Thomas Murphy, "you seem to be unusually uneasy."

"It's a very warm day," said Billy.

"If it seems hot to you in here," said Thomas Murphy, settling still further back in his chair, "what do you think it has been to me a-sittin' out under that canopy in the sun?"

Billy grew desperate. "Mr. Murphy," he said, "it seems to me—do you think, Mr. Murphy—I mean—don't you think that Mr. Prescott expects you are sitting out there now?"

"That may be," answered Thomas Murphy.

"Don't you think," said Billy, growing more and more desperate, "that it would be a good plan for us to go out there together?"

"Sometimes," said Thomas Murphy, in an injured tone, "a man's best friends can make things very hard for him."

"Can I help you to get up?" asked Billy, going up to Thomas Murphy, and putting his hand on his arm.

"No, William," said Thomas Murphy, moving his arm with more decision than was really necessary. "Thomas Murphy is still able to rise without the assistance of a—a friend."

Slowly Thomas Murphy drew himself from the depths of the chair.

Billy, backing out the great door, saw the clock.

Ten minutes more gone!

"Hurry up!" said William Wallace. "Hurry up!"

"I tell you, Mr. Murphy," said Billy in his most friendly tone, "I'll go out under the canopy. Then, if Mr. Prescott does come out, he'll see that there's somebody at the gate."

"Very well," said Thomas Murphy, lowering his lame leg carefully down the step. "Very well."

Billy, glad of a chance to work off his feelings, ran out to the gate as fast as he could.

Slowly, very slowly, Thomas Murphy came across the yard.

Billy, that he might not seem to be watching, stood with his back to the mill.

About the time that he thought Thomas Murphy would reach the gate, he heard a sudden exclamation. Turning around, he saw Thomas Murphy, timekeeper of Prescott mill, lying flat on his face.

Quarter-past four stood the hands of the clock. Never in his life had Billy seen them move so fast at that time of the day.

Hurrying back he asked, "Can I help you, Mr. Murphy?"

"Thank you, William," answered Thomas Murphy, holding out his hand for help. "A friend in need is a friend indeed."

As Billy bent over to help Thomas Murphy, he saw something that, for a moment, made him so excited that he couldn't have told whether he was standing on his head or his heels.

A black-haired man was creeping along the wall toward the door of the mill!

When he was sure that he was standing on his heels, Billy looked at the clock.

Seven minutes left!

He helped Thomas Murphy to his chair. He even took

time to say, "Mr. Murphy, there are some things that I have been wanting to ask you about iron."

"Anything," said Thomas Murphy, safe in his chair, "anything that I know is at your service, William."

Then Billy said, "Mr. Prescott told me to come back at half-past four."

"I should say," remarked Thomas Murphy, "that you'll have to hurry, William. Near as I can see the hands of that clock, it's hard on to that now."

Billy did hurry, and soon had the key safe in his hands.

As he went quickly down the corridor, William Wallace gave him some special advice:

"Don't explain. Business is business. Just deliver the key."

When Billy went into the office, Mr. Prescott glanced at the clock.

"Punctuality, William," he said, "is a desirable thing in business."

He took the key just as if he had been expecting it.

"Thank you, William," he said.

Then, seeming to forget Billy, he began to look the key over, stem, bit, and bow, touching it here and there, and holding it carefully, as if it were something that he valued very much.

Realizing, at last, that Billy was waiting, he said:

"Surprise, as I was saying, is one of the elements that must be reckoned with in business."

When he said that, he used his firm, business tone. But his voice was very gentle as he looked straight into Billy's eyes, and added:

"This time, William, the surprise is mine."

CHAPTER VII

IRON CUTS IRON

BOUT the middle of the next forenoon, as Billy was going through the gate, Thomas Murphy leaned forward confidentially, and said: "William, that key was in that door when I went to lock it last night."

"Yes," said Billy, hurrying on, "I saw it there when I went home."

Billy didn't care to discuss the matter.

The truth was that he thought it very strange that Mr. Prescott should have put the key right back in the lock. Business seemed to him to have some queer places in it.

But it had pleasant places, too, for, when Billy came back, he met Mr. Prescott, just starting on his trip around the mill.

"William," he said, "when a boy makes practical use of a visit to a foundry, I think it would be a good idea for him to go over a mill, don't you?"

That was a long speech for Mr. Prescott. There wasn't any time lost, however, for Billy didn't answer. He didn't have to, because his face told, right away, what he thought about it.

Miss King, looking up, nodded and smiled.

Off they went: tall, broad man; boy that was growing taller and slenderer every day.

Billy threw back his shoulders, and drew a long, deep breath. Part of it was satisfaction, the rest was a desire to be strong and broad like Mr. Prescott.

"That," said Mr. Prescott, as they passed a huge drum which was turning over and over and making a great-noise, "is a rattler. There's some sand left on castings after molding. Put small ones in there with pieces of wood. Rub each other off."

Mr. Prescott went on, seeming to forget Billy, as he spoke here and there to his men.

Billy followed close, for he knew that Mr. Prescott was likely, any moment, to spring a question on him.

They were halfway over the mill before Mr. Prescott spoke again. Then, stopping suddenly before a large lathe, he said: "John Bradford makes our best beds and slides. See him?" he asked, turning to Billy.

"He was making something long," answered Billy.

"We make lathes," said Mr. Prescott. "Good ones, all kinds."

In the next room he stopped again.

"Different kinds of iron," he said. "Some much harder than others, like tool steel. Iron cuts iron. That's a planing machine: automatic plane cuts any thickness."

Billy stopped beside the mighty planer, moving over the large casting as easily as if the iron had been wood and the fierce chisel only a carpenter's plane.

They went on a little further, then Mr. Prescott turned suddenly. "William," he asked, "how long is an inch?"

He certainly had sprung it on Billy, but Billy's spring worked too.

"About down to there," he answered, marking his left forefinger off with his right. "No," he said, moving his mark up a little higher, "about there."

"You were nearer right the first time," said Mr. Prescott. "Now, listen to me. Iron can cut iron to within a fraction of a thousandth of an inch."

Billy's eyes opened till they showed almost twice as much white as blue.

"Look at that," he said a moment later. "See that machine cutting a screw."

That seemed to be something that especially interested Mr. Prescott, for he stood a moment to watch the tool that was cutting into the round bar of iron, making, in even and regular grooves, a huge screw. Automatically, too, there came down on it a steady stream of oil.

"Why's that?" asked Billy.

"The oil keeps the iron from becoming too hot," answered Mr. Prescott. "Heat expands iron. If we didn't keep it cool, the screw wouldn't be the right size when it is done.

"Cold naturally works the other way. Ever hear about the iron bridge where the parts wouldn't quite come together, so they put ice on to do the job?" he asked, but he kept right on, without waiting for Billy to answer.

Billy saw other machines boring holes and rounding corners. It seemed as if iron could cut iron into any shape that anybody wanted.

Then there were men polishing and polishing, until they could fairly see their faces in the iron. Billy could hardly

There Were Men Polishing And Polishing

believe that the gray iron of the foundry could ever have become such silver-shining iron.

Still Mr. Prescott kept on, Billy close behind.

"This," said Mr. Prescott, stopping in a room almost at the end of the mill, "is the assembly room. Here is where the machines are put together.

"Over there," he said, pointing across the room, "they are putting a lathe together. There will be between sixty and seventy pieces in it when it is done. See, they have arranged all the parts."

Billy looked wonderingly at the great base and slide, and then at the rods and screws and handles and nuts. He didn't see how anybody could tell how they went together.

When he asked Mr. Prescott, he said: "They have drawings that they follow till the men can do it almost without referring to the drawing."

"What's that?" asked Billy, pointing to a queer thing over beyond the lathe.

"That," answered Mr. Prescott, "is one of our special orders. It is a corn canning machine."

Billy's eyes grew so bright that Mr. Prescott said: "Do corn canners interest you more than lathes?"

"That's what Uncle John was making the day that I went to watch him; he made some of the knives."

"Here they are," said Mr. Prescott, "where they were made to go. I think, myself, that this is rather an interesting machine. They put the corn in at one end, and it comes out in cans at the other, and nobody touches it."

"It's wonderful," said Billy, going over once more to look at the parts of a lathe that were assembled, ready to be put together, "how all the parts fit, when so many different people make them."

"If every man in this world would do his work as faithfully as our men do, things in the world would fit together much better than they do," said Mr. Prescott.

That sounded like Uncle John. It was the first time that Billy had thought that Mr. Prescott and Uncle John were a little alike.

A moment later, Mr. Prescott pushed back a sliding door, and they both went into the new part of the mill.

"This," said Mr. Prescott, "is to be the new assembly room. We have needed it for a long time. I shall be glad when it is done."

Then he turned so suddenly that he almost ran into Billy.

"Any questions, William?" he asked.

Billy's face must have given his answer again, for Mr. Prescott pushed an empty box toward Billy. Finding one for himself he turned it over, and, sitting down opposite him, said: "Fire away."

"What," asked Billy, "is the difference between iron and steel?"

"If you were to put that question as it ought to be put," answered Mr. Prescott, pushing his box against the wall, and leaning back with his hands in his pockets, "you would ask what is the difference between irons and steels.

"If I were to talk all day, I couldn't fully answer that question; but perhaps I can clear things up for you just a little.

"In the first place, every mining region produces its own variety of ore—so there are a great many kinds of iron to start with. In the next place, the kind of iron that you get from the ore depends largely on how you treat it.

"I suppose that you have seen a blacksmith shoe horses, haven't you?"

"Yes," answered Billy. "I knew a blacksmith up in the country."

"Well," said Mr. Prescott, "how did he work

"He heated the shoe red-hot on the forge, and then hammered it into shape on the anvil."

"Blew bellows, didn't he?" queried Mr. Prescott.

"Sure," answered Billy. "Sometimes he used to let me do that."

"Well, then," said Mr. Prescott, "just remember three things: fuel, blast, and hammer—power, of course, behind the hammer. It's the different variations that men have been making on those three things that have brought iron where it is today.

"Iron ore has so many things besides iron in it that the problem has always been how to get the impurities out.

"The old blacksmiths used to put it in the fire and hammer it; put it back in the fire and hammer again, until they worked most of the other things out. They made what is called forge iron.

"Then an Englishman, named Cort, found a way to burn and roll the impurities out. The thing they particularly wanted to get rid of was carbon, because that makes iron too brittle to use for a great many things.

"They worked away till a man—Sir Henry Bessemer—found a way to burn out all the carbon, and to make a kind of steel called Bessemer steel.

"Steel is, technically, an alloy of iron and carbon. The point is to have the carbon added to the iron in just the right proportion to make the kind of steel that you may happen to want.

"Bessemer—he was an Englishman, too—invented a converter to put carbon back into iron, that is, to make iron into steel.

"When it comes to telling you about steels, I can't do that to-day, there are too many kinds.

"You may not know it, William, but you are living in the age of steel. Industry depends on iron, for almost all the tools in the world are made of steel.

"Cast iron, like ours, is more brittle than steel, because it has much more carbon in it; but it is useful for many things. I shall stand right by cast iron."

Then he said, half to himself:

"Sometimes I wish the other fellows hadn't discovered quite so much. I should have liked to have a hand in it myself."

Then Billy put the question that he had been trying to find a chance to ask.

"Mr. Prescott," he began, but stopped a moment, as though he were having some difficulty in getting his question into shape. "Do volcanoes ever throw up mountains of iron?"

"Trying to get back to the beginning, are you?" asked Mr. Prescott. "Planning to be a geologist?"

But seeing that Billy was too serious, just then, to be put off lightly, Mr. Prescott went on:

"That's a good question. The geologists tell us, and I suppose that they are right, that there was once a chain of active volcanoes up in the Lake Superior region, and that is why there is so much iron up there now.

"There are some volcanoes in the world now, but the volcanoes that the geologists talk about became extinct—dead, you know—long before the earth was ready for man. Nobody knows how many thousands of years ago.

"Noon!" he exclaimed, as the whistle blew. "What a short morning this has been!"

As soon as Billy could get to Uncle John he told him where he had been.

"I thought," said Uncle John, nodding his head, "that that chance would come some day, Billy. Watch for a chance, and it generally comes."

Not until Billy went out the gate that night did he have an opportunity to speak to Thomas Murphy.

He let Uncle John go on a few steps ahead, then he said in a low tone: "Mr. Murphy, there were volcanoes out there geologists say so; but they're dead; been dead thousands of years."

Thomas Murphy, listening with eager ears, looked gravely into Billy's eyes. "All of 'em, everywhere?" he asked earnestly.

"Those old volcanoes," answered Billy, so impressed with Tom's seriousness that he made each word stand out by itself, "are all dead, everywhere."

The look of relief that came into Tom's face almost startled Billy.

Then, seeing that Uncle John was waiting for him, Billy said quickly "Just as soon as I can get a chance, Mr. Murphy, I want you to tell me some more of the things that you know about iron."

Thomas Murphy, suddenly freed from his fear, straightened up as, with the air of an expert, he said: "That's a large subject, William."

"You and Tom Murphy," said Uncle John, when Billy overtook him, "seem to be pretty good friends."

"I promised to tell him something," said Billy.

But that was all he said, for just as truly as Thomas Murphy knew that work is work, did Billy Bradford know that secrets are secrets.

CHAPTER VIII

TRAITOR NAILS

OR several days Billy was so busy that he had to resist all of Tom Murphy's attempts to make him stop to talk.

Then one noon, as he was going through the gate, Tom said: "Why don't you bring your dinner out here, William? Then we can have that talk about iron."

Much as he wanted to be with Uncle John, Billy really was anxious to hear what Thomas Murphy had to say about iron. So he answered: "I think, Mr. Murphy, that that would be a good plan."

When Billy came back, Thomas Murphy, eager of his opportunity, was putting the cover on his own pail.

Then, sitting up straight in his chair, and swelling with oratorical pride, he began: "William, I told you that iron is a large subject. The more a man thinks about it, the larger it gets.

"Here," he said, waving his left hand, "is our mill. What do we make? We make lathes, corn canners, and—and—all sorts of things. What do we make them of? Iron.

"What carries them all over the country? Iron engines. What do those engines run on, William? Iron rails. What carries 'em across the ocean? Iron ships.

"What makes our flour? Iron grinding machines.

"What heats our houses? Iron stoves. What—"

Pausing a moment for breath, he thrust his thumbs under his suspenders. Happening to hit the buckles, he began again: "What holds our clothes together? Iron buckles, iron buttons," he said with emphasis.

Pausing again, he looked up.

"What," he said, pointing dramatically at the telephone wire, "carries our messages from land to land, from shore to shore? Iron."

He paused again. Seeing that he had Billy's attention, Tom looked at him a moment in silence.

"William," he said so suddenly that Billy fairly jumped, "those very shoes that you are a-standin' in are held together by iron nails!"

Then, leaning forward, with his elbows resting on the arms of his chair, he concluded: "William, as far as I can see, if it wasn't for iron, we should all be just nothin', nobody."

Billy, drawing a long breath, said: "You've certainly done a lot of thinking, Mr. Murphy."

"I thank you, William," said Thomas Murphy, "for a-seein' and a-sayin' that I've been a-thinkin'."

Tom had set Billy to thinking, too. By night there were several things that Billy wanted to know.

It was so hot that Aunt Mary surprised them by setting the table out in the hall. There wasn't room for them to sit at the table, so she handed them the things out on the steps.

"That was a good idea, Mary," said Uncle John, when they were through. "I'm glad that you worked that out."

Billy, looking up into her face, said: "It was real nice, Aunt Mary."

Aunt Mary smiled. Billy, watching her, thought that her smile had moved just a little further out on her face. So he said again: "It was real nice, Aunt Mary."

Was he wrong, or did her smile move still a little further out?

"Uncle John," said Billy, "are ships made of iron?"

"Why, Billy, you're not going to sail away from us, are you?" said Uncle John, almost unconsciously putting his hand on Billy's. "Ships are made of steel."

"Mr. Prescott," said Billy, "explained to me about steel, and about forges."

"When this country was first settled," said Uncle John, "men had little forges to make iron, just as their wives had spinning wheels to make wool for clothes.

"When they began to make nails—they couldn't build houses without nails—there was a forge in almost every chimney corner. Children, as well as grown people, used to make nails and tacks in the long winter evenings. People then took nails to the store to pay for things, as in the country they now take eggs.

"That old forge iron was never very pure. It did the work that they had to do, but the world needed better iron, and more of it. It took a good while to find out a better way. The men that finally succeeded worked hard and long. You ought to begin to read up about those men.

"Of course it closed out a good many blacksmiths, but it

helped the world along. Guess they found, in the end, that it helped them along, too."

Then Billy told Uncle John what Thomas Murphy had said about being "nothin' and nobody." Aunt Mary came out to know what they were laughing about, so he told her the story.

"Mind you, Billy," said Uncle John, "I'm only laughing at the way he put it. Murphy is right. He seems to be unusually clear on the usefulness of iron."

Only a day or two later Billy had occasion to remember what Tom Murphy had said about the nails in his shoes.

In spite of all his efforts to grow broad, Billy was growing taller and slimmer every day. His legs were getting so long and his trousers so short, that Billy was beginning to wish that he could have some new clothes. But that wasn't his greatest worry.

There generally is one worry on top. This time it was shoes. They were growing short, but, worse than that, the sole of the right one was beginning to look as if it were coming off at the toe.

He and Aunt Mary looked at it every morning, for she hadn't quite money enough for a new pair. Uncle John still made Billy put his money in the bank—"Against a rainy day," Uncle John said.

Billy had tried, as hard as he could, to favor his right shoe. Of course he couldn't walk quite even: it made him hop a little. But he had only two days more to wait, and he thought that he could manage it.

Probably he would have succeeded, if it hadn't happened that Mr. Prescott needed some change. He told Billy to "sprint" to the bank for three rolls of dimes and two rolls of nickels.

Billy made good time on his way to the bank, handed in his five-dollar bill, took his five rolls of money, and started back.

He made good time on his way back until he reached the bridge, about three minutes' walk from the mill gate. Then he hit a board that had been put on as a patch, and off came that right sole, so that it went flop—flop—flop.

He had to hold his feet very high in order to walk at all; but he flopped along, until he stubbed his left toe and fell down flat.

The fall was so hard that it threw one roll of dimes out of his pocket. Just as he had stretched out till he almost had the roll, it began to turn over and over, and went off the edge of the bridge into the river. Billy saw it go.

Pulling himself up quickly, he put both hands into his pockets to hold the rest of the money in, and hurried on as fast as he could.

As he flopped through the gate, he half heard Tom Murphy say: "Those nails kinder went back on you, didn't they, William?"

When Mr. Prescott took the money, Billy held up his foot so that Mr. Prescott could see his shoe, then he told him about the money.

Mr. Prescott seemed to take in the situation, and he seemed not to mind much about the money, for he said: "We shall have to charge that up to profit and loss."

Billy found a piece of string to tie his sole on, and, that very night, as soon as he got home, Aunt Mary gave him a pair of new, rubber-soled shoes.

That was Thursday. The next Monday—Mr. Prescott paid the men on Monday—when Mr. Prescott gave Billy his little brown envelope, Billy said: "If you please, sir, I shall feel better if you will take out the dollar that I lost."

Then something happened. It seems as though Satan must have got into Mr. Prescott's mind, and must have had, for a moment, his own wicked way. That seems to be the only way to explain how a man like Mr. Prescott could say such a thing as he did to a boy like Billy.

Mr. Prescott thought that Billy said, "I shall feel better" because his conscience was troubling him. He looked down at Billy's new shoes. "New shoes," he said rather gruffly.

It didn't sound a bit like Mr. Prescott.

Billy wanted to tell him how long Aunt Mary had been saving up money to buy those shoes, but he had been practicing so hard on keeping his lips shut that he didn't say anything.

"Take your envelope," said Mr. Prescott.

After Billy had started for the door, Mr. Prescott added: "I rather think that the firm can stand a pair of shoes."

Billy's back was toward him. Perhaps, if he had been looking right at Billy, he wouldn't have said it, but say it he did.

Billy didn't, just then, take it in. He said, "Good-bye, Mr. Prescott," as he always did when he went home.

Miss King's keys kept going—clickety—clickety—click.

There was another side to it. When a good man like Mr. Prescott grows interested in a boy, and, about the time when he feels pretty sure that the boy is all right, something happens, especially about money, the man feels terribly. Then any man is likely to say hard things.

Billy had never even heard about such a thing as 'conscience money,' but Mr. Prescott had had an experience with a man whose conscience didn't work at the right time.

Billy felt uncomfortable when he went out the door; but he was fully half-way home before he realized that Mr. Prescott thought that he had told a lie about the roll of dimes; thought that he had—Billy couldn't finish that sentence.

He hardly spoke to Uncle John all the way home. Then, though Aunt Mary had a special treat—the little cakes covered with white frosting, the kind that Billy liked best—he could hardly eat one.

He felt worse and worse. Of course Uncle John knew that something was wrong, but he knew that a boy can't always talk about his heartaches. Then, if it were business, he didn't want to tempt him to tell. So Uncle John didn't ask any questions.

They sat on the steps a long time—so much longer than usual that Aunt Mary called: "William Wallace, it's time to come in."

When she said that, Uncle John said he was so thirsty that he should have to go in to get some water.

Billy heard Uncle John call Aunt Mary into the kitchen to find him a glass. Then he came out again and sat down close by Billy.

They sat there till long after the clock struck nine. Then Billy said: "Uncle John, if anybody thought something b—b—something about you, and it wasn't so, what would you do?"

"I would," answered Uncle John, slowly, "keep right on working, and leave that to God."

Then he put his arm around Billy's shoulders, drew him up close, and said again, slowly, "I would leave that to God."

After they had sat a minute longer, they both went into the house.

Billy wished that night, even more than usual, that he

and Uncle John might say their prayers together, the way he and his father used to do. But he did the best he could alone.

He said his prayers very slowly and very carefully. Then he said them all over again, and climbed into bed.

After the house was dark, Billy heard Uncle John come to his door. Billy didn't speak, but he heard Uncle John say something. Perhaps, though he said it very softly, Uncle John hoped that he would hear him when he said softly, "Eh, Billy, little lad!"

CHAPTER IX

BILLY STANDS BY

HEN Miss King came into the office the next morning, she had a large bunch of bachelor's buttons in her hand. They were blue—all shades of blue—and they looked very pretty against the clear white of her dress. She had hardly taken off her hat before the telephone rang hard.

Billy heard her say, "Yes, Mr. Prescott."

"Mr. Prescott says he's not coming to the office till after lunch," she said, turning to Billy. "It's something about the new part of the mill.

"We got along all right the other day, didn't we? I was anxious all for nothing, wasn't I, William?

"Now, please get me some water for the flowers, and we'll settle down to work."

Billy didn't feel, that morning, much like talking to anybody, not even to Miss King, so he didn't say anything.

When he brought back the tall glass vase, Miss King took three of the bluest flowers and broke off the stems.

"I should like to put these in your buttonhole, William," she said. "They'll look pretty against your gray coat.

"August is late for bachelor's buttons; we shall have to make the most of these. Really," she went on, as she fastened them with a pin on the underside of his lapel, "they're just the color of your eyes."

Miss King didn't usually say very much. It was a surprise to Billy to have her keep on talking.

"How nice the office looks, William! We never had a boy before that knew how to dust in anything but streaks."

"My Aunt Mary," said Billy, speaking at last, "is very particular. She showed me how to dust."

Then Miss King sorted the orders, and Billy started out with them.

It was still very hot. The latest thing that Mr. Prescott had done to try to make the office a little cooler was to move a pile of boxes and to open an old door at the other end of the corridor opposite the door with the great key.

That door hadn't been opened for a long time. Hardly anybody had realized that there was a door on that side. It opened over the end of an old canal that had been used in his grandfather's day. Filling up that "old ditch," as Mr. Prescott called it, was one of the things that he was planning to do.

When he had the door opened, he put up a danger notice, and left in place, across the door, an old beam that had once been used as a safety guard.

Billy stood in the corridor a moment, and looked back through the old door. If it ever rained, that would be a pretty view.

But the old willow beyond the ditch was green on one

side, even if it was dead on the other where its branches stuck out like—like—

Billy, trying to decide what they did look like, began, almost unconsciously, to walk toward the door.

By the time that he decided that the branches looked like the antlers of two great deer, standing with their heads close together, Billy reached the door.

He stood a moment looking down at the old canal. He was surprised to see how far below the door the canal really lay. The dry spot at the end had some ugly stones in it, too. Just as well to have a place like that filled in.

Looking again at the old willow, Billy turned and went slowly back down the corridor and out the great door.

When Mr. Prescott finally came back, Billy was on his afternoon rounds.

Things were very quiet, but that was to be expected at that time of the day.

Were things unusually quiet?

Just then Mr. Prescott heard a faint cry. In an instant he was at the door.

Somebody was crying, "Fire!"

Who was he? Where was he? Why didn't he call louder?

He met Billy, who was fairly flying back from the other end of the yard, with his hands at his throat as if he were trying to make the sound come out.

"The new part is on fire!" he cried; "the new part of the mill is on fire!"

Mr. Prescott rushed to the fire alarm.

Billy kept on to the office and burst in, crying, "The new part is on fire!"

Miss King started for the door. Mr. Prescott had given her orders what to do if there ever should be a fire.

Billy himself was partway down the corridor when something in his head began to say faintly:

"Stand—by—your—job—every—minute—that—you—belong—on—it!"

Though Billy slowed down a little, he did not stop, but kept right on until he reached the door, and had one foot out.

Then the graphophone in his mind began again, a little louder than before:

"Stand—by—your—job—every—minute—that—you—belong—on—it!"

Billy drew his foot back. He felt as though he must do something, so he shut the great door. He turned and stood against it for a minute. Then he started slowly down the corridor.

The graphophone had stopped; but Billy's quick ears heard another sound. Somebody was trying to open the great door!

Billy remembered the little closet. He could see the office from that. He hurried on, and had barely slipped into it when the door opened.

In came the man with the fierce black eyes and the coal black hair, and he was carrying something in both hands.

Billy fairly held his breath. The door was a little too far open, but he didn't dare to touch it.

The door was too far open. It was open so far that, hitting it as he passed, the man gave it an angry kick.

The door went to so hard that Billy heard the click of the spring lock as it fastened the door, and made him a prisoner in the closet.

Keep still he must till the man was out of the way. That

was the only thing to do. Billy took out his jack-knife. It felt friendly, so he opened it.

Sooner than he expected he heard the man come out, heard him go heavily down the corridor, and heard him close the great door.

Cracks between the boards let in light enough for Billy to find the lock. He began to pry away at it with his knife. He thought he had started it a little, when snap went the blade.

Then he tried the other, working a little more carefully; but, in a moment, snap went that blade, broken close to the handle.

He tried kicking the boards where he saw the largest cracks, but not a board could he move.

Then he grew so excited that he hardly knew what he was doing.

What was going on in the office? Was that on fire? He threw himself against the sides of the closet, one after the other.

He wasn't sure whether it was his head or the closet that began to rock. It seemed to be the closet.

Once more he threw himself against the back of the closet. That time he was sure it was the closet that rocked!

He threw himself three times, four times, five times. Suddenly he landed on his head in the top of the closet on a heap of clothes. Light was coming in from somewhere. His head was rocking so that he could hardly move, but, in a minute, he managed to turn and to crawl out of the bottom of the closet, where the cleats had given way.

It was easier, just then, for him to crawl than it was to walk. So he crawled across to the office, reached up, and opened the door.

Surprised he certainly was, for everything seemed to be all right.

Billy, beginning to feel pretty sore in several places, pulled himself up into Mr. Prescott's chair.

Then he heard a faint tick, tick, tick.

No, it wasn't the clock. Billy had kept his ears open too long not to know that.

Where was it? What was it? It seemed very near!

Billy looked under the desk. Nothing there but the waste basket.

His heart was going thump, thump. But, when a boy is standing by his job, he doesn't stop for a thumping heart.

Billy didn't. He took hold of the basket. It was very heavy. The ticking was very near.

Then Billy knew!

It was what Uncle John called an "infernal machine," with clockworks inside!

Billy dug down among the papers till he found the thing. He took it in both hands and pulled it out—it was a sort of box. He started for the door. All he could think of was that he must take the infernal thing away from Mr. Prescott's desk.

Out he went with it. The old door was still open. Billy, holding the box in his arms, made a frantic dash for the door.

When he reached it, he leaned against the old beam and, gathering all his strength, threw the box over into the old dry ditch. He heard the box fall.

Then, with a creaking sound, the old beam broke from its rusty fastenings and followed the box.

After that there was another fall, for the boy that had thrown the box went down with the beam.

But that was a fall that Billy did not hear.

CHAPTER X

WILLIAM WALLACE

HE next thing that Billy knew he was waking up, not wide awake, but a little at a time. The room seemed very white, and there was somebody in white standing by his bed. No, it wasn't Miss King, for this woman had something white on her head. Then he felt somebody holding his hand and saying, "Billy, little Billy."

He woke up a little further. He tried to say, "Aunt Mary," but the words wouldn't come. The woman in white took hold of Aunt Mary, and led her out of the room. Then he saw something large in the window. He wasn't at all sure that he wasn't dreaming about mountains. But this mountain had a round top and, while he watched it, it moved. Billy woke up enough to see that it was somebody standing in the window.

Billy knew only one person who could fill up a window like that. He tried his voice again. This time he made it go.

"That you, Mr. Prescott?" he said, his voice going up and up till it ended in a funny little quaver.

68

Then the mountain came over to him. It was Mr. Prescott.

Billy, looking up, spoke again, very slowly: "The dimes did roll into the river, Mr. Prescott."

"Hang it!" said Mr. Prescott. "Of course they did!"

The nurse nodded. "He's kept talking about that," she said. "We thought perhaps you'd know."

Mr. Prescott started to go close to the bed.

The nurse put out her hand.

"Hang it!" said Mr. Prescott. "I was a brute. Can you ever forgive me, Billy?"

"Sure, sir," answered Billy.

His voice sounded so strong that the nurse told Mr. Prescott that she was afraid he was exciting the patient.

Billy said, "Please stay."

Then the nurse told Mr. Prescott that he might stay ten minutes if he wouldn't talk to the patient.

Billy tried to smile at Mr. Prescott, but he was so tired that he shut his eyes instead.

Next time it was Uncle John who was holding his hand, but Uncle John didn't smile.

"Uncle John," said Billy, "what's the matter with me?"

"Just a few broken bones, Billy, my lad," answered Uncle John.

"Which ones?" asked Billy.

"Just a left arm and a left leg."

"That all?" asked Billy.

After that they wouldn't let him see anybody. There were two nurses instead of one, and three doctors—"specialists" Billy heard his own nurse say.

After that there were two doctors every day—a doctor

with white hair, and a doctor with light brown hair, parted in the middle. The doctor with the white hair seemed to think more about Billy than he did about his bones, for he talked to Billy while he was feeling around.

The young doctor seemed to think more about the bones. But Billy liked him, too, for one day when they were hurting him terribly the young doctor said: "You're a game sort of chap."

Billy wasn't quite sure what "game" meant, but he kept right on gritting his teeth till they were through.

The first day that the young doctor began to come alone, he said: "Nurse, how are the contusions getting along?"

"They are much lighter in color, doctor, this morning," answered the nurse.

"I don't understand," said the doctor, standing very straight and putting his forefinger on his chin, "how a fall of the nature of this one, practically on the left side, could have produced so many contusions on the right."

"What are contusions?" asked Billy.

The doctor began to talk about stasis of the circulation following superficial injuries.

"Show me one," said Billy.

When the nurse showed him one on his right arm, just below the shoulder, Billy said: "Oh, one of my black and blue spots! That must have been when I was playing caged lion."

That time the doctor and the nurse were the ones who didn't understand.

Then Billy laughed, a happy boyish laugh. He hadn't laughed that way since he and his father used to have frolics together.

The doctor looked at him a minute, then he said: "Nurse, to-morrow this young chap may have company for half an hour."

"I'm glad to hear that, doctor," said the nurse. "I'll go right away to tell Mr. Prescott. He's fairly worn me out with telephoning to know when we would let him come."

At ten o'clock the next morning Mr. Prescott came.

After he had answered Billy's questions about the fire, and had told him that the new roof was almost finished, he took a newspaper out of his pocket. He folded it across, then down on both sides, and held it up in front of Billy.

There it was, in big head-lines:

"BILLY BRADFORD SAVES PRESCOTT MILL"

Then Mr. Prescott read him what the paper said. They had even put in about finding him with the flowers in his buttonhole.

"Those," interrupted Billy, "were Miss King's flowers."

"Yes," said Mr. Prescott; "she cried, right in the office, when she read that."

Then Billy told Mr. Prescott about the closet, and all about the box, and asked him to pull out the drawer in the little stand by his bed. There lay his jack-knife. Somebody had shut up all that was left of the blades, and there was so little left that they couldn't be opened.

Mr. Prescott put the knife into Billy's hand.

"That was a good knife," said Billy, looking at it with affection.

"I think," said Mr. Prescott, "that you really ought to let me have that knife."

Billy hesitated a moment, then he said:

"If you please, Mr. Prescott, I should like to keep that knife. It has been a good friend to me."

Mr. Prescott took the little white hand, knife and all, in his own strong, firm fingers.

"I want it, Billy, because you have been a good friend to me."

Billy's face flushed so suddenly red that Mr. Prescott was afraid that something was going to happen to Billy. He called, "Nurse—"

"I'm all right," said Billy.

He grew red again as he said:

"Mr. Prescott, I want to tell you something."

Mr. Prescott said: "Let me fix your pillows first."

Of course he got them all mixed up, and the nurse had to come. She looked at her watch, and then at Mr. Prescott, but she didn't say anything.

Then Mr. Prescott sat close by the bed with Billy's hand lying in his, and Billy told him about William Wallace.

Mr. Prescott looked a little surprised, then he said:

"William Wallace seems to know a good deal, doesn't he?"

Billy, in honor, had to nod his head, but he grew very sober. Perhaps, after all, Mr. Prescott would like William Wallace better than he liked him.

"I don't really approve," said Mr. Prescott, "of his calling you a coward, though that sometimes makes a boy try to be brave.

"One thing is sure, he can't ever call you that again, can he?"

Billy shook his head.

"Personally," continued Mr. Prescott, almost as if he were

talking business, "I had rather be saved by you than by William Wallace. Can you guess why?"

Billy shook his head again, but this time he smiled.

"Because," said Mr. Prescott, "you did it out of your heart. William Wallace would have done it out of his head."

Billy smiled serenely. Everything—broken jack-knife, broken arm, broken leg—was exactly all right now.

"Really and truly," Mr. Prescott went on, "there are two of everybody, only most people don't seem to know it, one is his heart, and the other is his head.

"If I were you, I would be on good terms with William Wallace—it generally takes both to decide. I'd take him as a sort of brother, but I wouldn't let him rule."

"No," said Billy.

Then Mr. Prescott saw the nurse coming, and he hurried off.

The next time that Uncle John came Billy asked him what had become of the man—"the poor man," Billy called him.

"That man," said Uncle John, his mouth growing rather firm, "was found out in his sin.

"He undertook a little too much when he set fire to one end of the mill, and then tried to blow up the main office. That's too much for one man to do at one time, especially when he's a man that leaves things around."

"Oh!" said Billy.

"Now," said Uncle John, "he's where he's having his actions regulated."

"I hope," said Billy, "that they'll be good to him."

"Billy," said Uncle John, very decidedly, "all that you are called upon to do about that man is to believe that he couldn't think straight.

"But the way this world is made makes it necessary, when a man can't think straighter than to try to destroy the very mill where he's working, for someone else to do a part of his thinking for him.

"That's what the men that make the laws are trying to do. They are trying to help men to think straight."

Billy was listening hard. It was a good while since he had heard one of Uncle John's lectures.

"You know, Billy, my lad, that there are a lot of things we have to leave to God."

"Yes, Uncle John."

"There are a lot more that we have to leave to the law.

"The best thing for a boy like you and a man like me to do is to leave things where they belong."

"All right, Uncle John, I will," said Billy, giving a little sigh of relief as if he were glad to have that off his mind.

The next day when Mr. Prescott came, he told Billy that, the day after that, he was to be moved to Mr. Prescott's house on the hill.

Billy looked a little sober. He had been thinking a great deal about home.

"I'm all alone in that big house," said Mr. Prescott.

"Then," said Billy, "I'll come."

CHAPTER XI

THE TREASURE ROOM

HEY took Billy to Mr. Prescott's house in his machine. They had to take a good many pillows and they planned to take an extra nurse, but the young doctor said that he was going up that way, and could just as well help. Billy and the doctor were getting to be very good friends.

"He's different," Billy had confided to Uncle John, "but I like him a lot."

"Nice people often are different," said Uncle John.

Billy was so much better that he had some fun, while they were putting him into the auto, about his "stiff half," as he called his left side.

"You just wait till I get that arm and that leg to working," he said. "They'll have to work over time."

They put him in a large room with broad windows, where he could look down on the river and across at the mountains. There was a large brass bed in the room, but Mr. Prescott had had a hospital bed sent up.

75

"You'd have hard work to find me in that bed," said Billy to the nurse, "wouldn't you?"

It was a beautiful room. One of the maids told Billy that it had been Mr. Prescott's mother's room, and that he had always kept it as she had left it. For the first week Billy feasted his eyes on color. The walls of the room were soft brown; the paint was the color of cream. There were two sets of curtains: one a soft old blue, and over that another hanging of all sorts of colors. It took Billy a whole day to pick out the pattern on those curtains.

There was a mahogany dressing table, and there was a wonderful rug—soft shades of rose in the middle, and ever so many shades of blue in the border. There was a fireplace with a shining brass fender. And there were—oh, so many things!

Then Billy spent almost another week on the pictures. But when he wanted to rest his eyes he looked at his old friends, the mountains, lying far across the river.

Mr. Prescott, too, liked the mountains. He came to sit by him in the evening, and they had real friendly times together watching the mountains fade away into the night, and seeing the electric lights flash out, one after another, all along the river.

Finally the doctors took off the splints. They had a great time doing it, testing his joints to see whether or not they would work. Then Billy found that, as the young doctor said, there had been a "tall lot of worrying done about those bones." This time the white-haired doctor paid more attention to his bones than he did to Billy. He didn't say anything till he went to put his glasses back in the case. Then he straightened up, and said:

"I'm happy to tell you, young man, that those joints will work all right after they get used to working again."

The next day Billy went down the long flight of stairs, with Mr. Prescott on one side, and the nurse on the other, to the great library, right under the room where he had been.

"Feel pretty well, now that you're down?" asked Mr. Prescott, after the nurse had gone upstairs.

"Sure, sir," answered Billy.

"Then follow me," said Mr. Prescott, opening a door at the end of the library.

Billy followed, but he had hardly stepped in before he stepped back.

"Why, Billy," said Mr. Prescott, coming quickly back to him, "I didn't mean to frighten you. We'll stay in the library."

Now the doctor had told Mr. Prescott that Billy mustn't be frightened by anything if they could help it, for he'd been through about all a boy's nerves could stand. So Mr. Prescott drew Billy over to the big sofa, fixed some pillows around him, and put a foot-rest under his leg. Then Mr. Prescott settled himself in a great chair as though he had nothing in the world to do except to talk to Billy.

"That," said Mr. Prescott, "is my treasure room. When I go in there, I think of brave men, and of how they helped the world along. What made you step back?"

"Because," answered Billy, half ashamed, "I thought I saw a man in the corner pointing something at me."

"I ought," said Mr. Prescott, "to have thought of that before I took you into the room.

"I've been trying, for some time, to make that old suit of armor and that spear look like a knight standing there, ready for action. I must have, at last, succeeded, but I'm sorry that it startled you.

"You see I'm naturally interested in weapons of war because they are all made of steel or iron."

"Battle-ships, too," said Billy.

"Yes," said Mr. Prescott. "But you mustn't forget the great naval battles that were won with ships of wood.

"There's one thing in that room," Mr. Prescott went on, "that I am sure you will like to see. It is my great-great-grandfather's musket."

"Oh," said Billy, "I didn't know that you had a great-great-grandfather."

"I did," said Mr. Prescott, just as quietly as if Billy had been talking sense. "He was a brave man, too. That is the musket that he had when he was with General Washington at Valley Forge."

"Oh!" exclaimed Billy again.

"Know about Valley Forge, do you?"

"A little," answered Billy, very humbly.

"That's enough to start on," said Mr. Prescott. Billy could almost imagine that Uncle John was talking. Billy spent a great deal more time every day than anybody realized in thinking about his Uncle John.

"Perhaps you don't know, many people don't," said Mr. Prescott, "that the first name of that place was Valley Creek. It was changed to Valley Forge because a large forge plant was established there. It was one of the first places in this state where they made iron and steel.

"By the way, George Washington's father was a maker of pig iron down in Virginia."

"Oh!" said Billy. "There seem to be a lot of things to know about iron."

"There's really no end to them," said Mr. Prescott. "They begin way back in history. Did you ever read about Goliath the giant?"

"My father used to read those stories to me," answered Billy, "out of a great big Bible."

"Was it like this one?" asked Mr. Prescott, getting up quickly and bringing him, from the library table, a great Bible, covered with light brown leather.

"That looks almost like ours," answered Billy.

"This," said Mr. Prescott, "is the one my mother used to read to me. There's a great deal about iron in it," he added, as he put it away carefully.

"To come back to Goliath," said Mr. Prescott. "His spear had a head of iron that weighed six hundred shekels.

"Then there was that iron bedstead of Og, king of Bashan. Ever hear of him?"

"I don't seem," answered Billy, "to remember about him."

"Perhaps I shouldn't have remembered," said Mr. Prescott, "if I hadn't been so interested in iron."

"That," said Billy, "was probably on account of your grandfather, and your father," he added quickly.

"There's a great deal about iron in the Bible," said Mr. Prescott. "Only four or five pages over in Genesis there is a verse about a man named Tubal-Cain, who was a master-worker in brass and iron.

"Then there are some things in mythology that you ought to know, now that you're interested in iron. One of them is that the old Romans, who imagined all sorts of gods, said that iron was discovered by Vulcan. They said, too, that he forged the thunderbolts of Jupiter.

"Now, then, Billy, how about my treasure room?"

"Ready, sir," answered Billy, working himself out from among his pillows.

"Once," said Mr. Prescott, walking close by Billy, "I went into a room something like this, only it had many more things in it. The room was in Sir Walter Scott's house. He had one of Napoleon's pistols from Waterloo.

"He called his room an armory. I generally call mine my 'treasure room.'"

"I think I like armory better," said Billy.

"Then," said Mr. Prescott, "will you walk into my armory?"

"First of all," said Billy, "I want to see that gun—musket."

"Here it is," said Mr. Prescott. "There," he added, pointing to a picture in an oval brass frame, "is my great-great-grandfather."

"Oh!" said Billy.

Then Mr. Prescott knew that Billy had never before seen a silhouette.

"That kind of picture," he said, "does make a man look as black as his own hat, though it is often a good profile. I used to make them myself. Some night I'll make one of you.

"Now that you've seen the musket, I think that you had better take a look at this suit of armor that I have been trying to make stand up here like a knight.

"This coat of mail is made of links, you see. Sometimes they were made of scales of iron linked together.

"The work that those old smiths did is really wonderful, especially when you remember that their only tools were hammer, pincers, chisel, and tongs. It took both time and patience to weld every one of those links together."

"I don't think I understand what weld means," said Billy.

"When iron is heated to a white heat," said Mr. Prescott, "it can be hammered together into one piece. Most metals have to be soldered, you know. The blacksmiths generally use a powder that will make the iron weld more easily, because it makes the iron soften more quickly, but iron is its own solder.

"You'd better sit down here while I explain a little about this suit of armor; then you'll know what you're reading about when you come to a knight.

"I suppose that every boy knows what a helmet and a vizor are, they learn about that from seeing firemen."

"And policemen," said Billy.

"Only the helmets of the knights covered their faces and ended in guards for their necks. I dare say that you don't know what a gorget is."

"No," said Billy, "I don't."

"That is the piece of armor that protected the throat. Here is the cuirass or breastplate, and the tassets that covered the thighs. They're hooked to the cuirass. And here are the greaves for the shins. There are names for all the arm pieces, too, but we'll let those go just now.

"This shield, you see, is wood covered with iron, and part of the handle inside is wood. A man must have weighed a great deal when he had a full suit of armor on, and he must have been splendid to look at and rather hard to kill.

"Those old smiths certainly made a fine art of their work in iron. They got plenty of credit for it, too. In the Anglo-Saxon times they were really treated as officers of rank.

"When a man was depending on his sword to protect his family, he naturally respected a man who could make good swords. The smiths sort of held society together."

Billy, looking around the room, saw that one side had spears and shields and helmets hung all over it; and on the wall at the end were pistols, bows and arrows, and some dreadful knives.

"Did all those," he asked, pointing at the end of the room, "kill somebody?"

"Ask it the other way," said Mr. Prescott; "did they all protect somebody? Then I can safely say that they did, for any foe would think twice before he attacked a man in mail. These things were all made because they were needed.

"What do you suppose put the armorers out of business?"

"I don't know," answered Billy.

"Gunpowder," said Mr. Prescott. "A man could be blown up, armor and all."

"Then they had to make guns," said Billy.

"And they've been at that ever since," said Mr. Prescott.

"Come over to this cabinet, and I'll show you my special treasure.

"Shut your eyes, Billy, and think of walls in a desert long enough and high enough to shut in a whole city."

Billy shut his eyes. "I see the walls," he said.

"Now, just inside the wall, think of a garden with great beds of roses."

"Blush roses?" queried Billy.

"Damask," replied Mr. Prescott; "pink, pretty good size."

"That's done!" said Billy.

"Now, in that garden, think an Arab chief, a sheik, mounted on a beautiful Arabian horse, and—open your eyes!"

"HERE IS HIS SWORD!"

"I saw him clearly!" exclaimed Billy, his eyes flying wide open. "My!" he said, "but that's a beauty!"

"It is," said Mr. Prescott. "Look!"

Then he took the hilt in his right hand and the point in his left, and began to bend the point toward the hilt.

"Don't," cried Billy. "You'll break it!"

"The tip and the hilt of the best of the old swords were supposed to come together," said Mr. Prescott. "See, this has an inscription in Arabic.

"I have a genuine Toledo, too, but you've been in here long enough. Let's go back into the library. You may come in here whenever you like. Mornings, I think, would be the best time."

When Billy was comfortably settled among his pillows, with the Damascus sword on the sofa by him, Mr. Prescott said: "Men, in the olden time, thought so much of their swords that they often named them, and had them baptized by the priest. The great emperor Charlemagne had a sword named 'Joyeuse.'

"Sometimes, too, the old bards sang about swords and their makers."

"Tell me," said Billy, "how they made swords."

"The people way over in the East understood the process of converting iron into steel, but in those days they had plenty of gold and very little steel, so swords were sometimes made of gold with only an edge of steel.

"The steel swords were made by hammering little piles of steel plates together. They were heated, hammered, and doubled over, end to end, until the layers of steel in a single sword ran up into the millions.

"Now, we'll come back to the present time, and I'll show you something that I brought home yesterday to put in my treasure room."

Billy watched eagerly, while Mr. Prescott took a package from the library table, and opened it. Then, in delight, he exclaimed: "The great iron key!"

"The same," said Mr. Prescott, "and glad enough I am to have it here. When I gave Tom the new key, he didn't look altogether happy. I think the fellow really has enjoyed having the care of this one."

"I suppose," said Billy, "that the new one is so small that he will be afraid of losing it. They don't make such large keys nowadays."

"That statement may be true in general," said Mr. Prescott, "but the fact is that the new key is as large as this."

Then Mr. Prescott stopped talking, but he looked right at Billy.

"You don't mean," said Billy, after thinking for a minute as hard as he could, "that you have had a key made, do you?"

"That is the meaning that I intended to convey," answered Mr. Prescott. "But I'm not going to tease a fellow that is downstairs for the first time, so I'll tell you, right away, that Mr. John Bradford made the casting for the new key, and he used this for a pattern."

"Oh!" said Billy, smiling.

"You didn't like it very well, did you, Billy," asked Mr. Prescott, "when I put that key back in the door?"

"No," answered Billy, "I didn't."

"Just at that time," said Mr. Prescott, "a great many things had to be considered. I decided that it was better to risk the key than to risk letting the man know that we knew what had happened.

"You never knew either, did you, how many nights after that I spent in the office?"

"Honest?" asked Billy, opening his eyes very wide.

"Running a mill, I'd have you understand, Billy Bradford," said Mr. Prescott, "is no easy job."

"It doesn't seem to be," said Billy, just as earnestly as if he had been a man.

"I must go," said Mr. Prescott. "I had almost forgotten that I am one of the modern workers in iron.

"Billy," he said suddenly, turning as he reached the door, "did you ever know anybody by the name of Smith?"

Billy's answer was a merry laugh.

"You needn't laugh, Billy Bradford," said Mr. Prescott. "If you do, perhaps I won't tell you something."

"Do," said Billy.

"People," said Mr. Prescott, coming partway back into the room, "didn't always have last names. When they came into fashion, all the workers on anvils were given Smith for a last name. That's where the Smiths came from!"

"Honest?" asked Billy.

"Fact," said Mr. Prescott, as he went through the door.

When the nurse came down a little later, she found Billy fast asleep among the cushions, and his hand was lying on the hilt of the Damascus blade.

THOMAS MURPHY, TIMEKEEPER

"HERE'S a garden," said Mr. Prescott, the next morning.

"Is there a garden?" interrupted Billy, eagerly.

"There's a garden," Mr. Prescott went on, in his steady, even tone, "down behind this house, and I have decided to give a garden party. Are there any ladies that you would like to invite?"

"All the ladies that I have in the world," said Billy, soberly, "are Aunt Mary and Miss King."

"Then invite them," said Mr. Prescott. "I think that, now you're well—"

Billy waved his arm, and thrust out his foot.

"Now you are well," continued Mr. Prescott, "it will be a good plan for you to have some company."

"When's that party going to be?" asked Billy, very eagerly.

"I thought," answered Mr. Prescott, "that perhaps we could manage it for to-morrow. Do you think it will be best to have the ladies alone, or shall we invite some men?"

"All the men I have," said Billy, "are Uncle John and the young doctor and Mr. Thomas Murphy."

"How would it do," said Mr. Prescott, "to have just your Aunt Mary and Miss King? Your Uncle John can come at any time. Perhaps you would enjoy Tom more if he were to come alone."

"I think," said Billy, reflectively, "that would be a good plan."

Then Billy told Mr. Prescott what Tom had said about being 'nothing and nobody.'

"That's good!" said Mr. Prescott, laughing. Then he added gravely, "Tom's a faithful man."

There was a garden. If Billy had ever dreamed about a garden, that would have been the garden of his dreams. Billy had never seen a garden like that.

It didn't show at all from the front of the house; neither could it be seen from Billy's windows; but there was a long garden with a round summer house at the end.

Because it was a city garden it had a high board fence on three sides. The fence was gray. Against it at the end, just behind the summer house, were rows of hollyhocks—pink, white, yellow, and rose—standing tall and straight, like sentinels on duty guard.

There were beds of asters, each color by itself, and great heaps of hydrangeas, almost tumbling over the lawn.

There were queer little trees. When Billy said that they looked like the trees on Japanese lanterns, Mr. Prescott said that they were real Japanese trees.

Billy didn't see the whole of that garden until after he had been in it a great many times. After he did see it all, it became the garden of his dreams.

The next afternoon Mr. Prescott sent the auto for Aunt Mary and Miss King, and they both came.

Billy had never seen Aunt Mary look so well. She had on a lavender and white striped muslin, with white lace and some tiny black velvet buttons on it. Uncle John liked to have her wear lavender.

Miss King had on a pretty white dress, a different kind from what she wore in the office. Her hat was white, trimmed with blue, and her white silk gloves went up to her elbows.

Billy took them out through the drawing-room balcony, and down the steps into the garden.

They didn't talk very much while they walked around, but a great deal of politeness went on in the garden that afternoon.

Aunt Mary smiled and kept calling him "Billy." He counted till he got up to ten times, then he was so busy showing them the flowers that he forgot to count.

When they went into the summer house where the waitress had set a little table, they all sat down on the same side. That brought Billy between Aunt Mary and Miss King.

He helped them to ice-cream and cakes. There really wasn't much helping to do, for the ice-cream was made like strawberries, leaves and all, only each one was about three times as large as strawberries grow.

They sat there a long time, keeping on being polite; but not a bit of the politeness was wasted, for they were all very happy when they were through.

Then Mr. Prescott came in the auto. After Aunt Mary and Miss King had gone, Mr. Prescott said that he should like a strawberry, so Billy had a chance to be polite to Mr. Prescott, too.

Altogether, Billy had a delightful party.

Mr. Prescott brought word that Thomas Murphy would come the next day, because that would be Saturday, and the mill would be closed in the afternoon.

Thomas Murphy came, clean-shaven, and dressed in his best.

"Well, William," he said, shaking Billy's hand hard, "how are you, William?"

"Don't you think, Mr. Murphy," said Billy, "that I look pretty well?"

"Better than I ever expected to see you, William, after that day."

"Mr. Prescott," said Billy, "thinks we'd better not talk very much about that."

"No, William," said Thomas Murphy, "we won't talk about the martyr side of it. But there's something we will talk about. That's why I've come. There are things, William, that you ought to know."

Seeing how warm Thomas Murphy was growing, Billy suggested that they had better go out into the garden.

"That's a good idea, William," said he, limping after Billy.

After he was settled in a comfortable garden chair, Thomas Murphy hung a handkerchief with a figured purple border over his knee, clasped his hands across his chest, and began again.

"William," he said solemnly, "while you were a-lyin' unconscious in that hospital, I was a-thinkin' about what you had asked me about bein' a friend to the super.

"Every time I read that bulletin that was posted every day on that door, 'unconscious still,' I thought some more.

"The day that said 'dangerous,' I finished thinkin'.

"Thomas Murphy, timekeeper, 'said I sharp, 'it's time that you did something more than mark time; it's time you found out whether you're a-markin' friends or foes.'

"When the men came in the next morning, they just filed past that bulletin. Then says I, Thomas Murphy, act. The time to act has come.'

"Somethin' in me said, 'Suppose you should be a martyr like William.'

"Suppose I be a martyr, 'said I. 'Am I a-goin' to have William a-lyin' dangerous, and a man like me a-sittin' still?'

Billy moved in his chair, and Thomas Murphy paused for breath.

"That noon," he continued, "I told Peter Martin to blow the whistle three times. The super a-bein' at the hospital, I gave the order myself. What do three whistles mean, William"

"All men come to the gate," answered Billy promptly.

"They came," said Thomas Murphy. "I got up on a box, so I could see the whole of 'em. Men, 'said I, 'that boy, William, is lyin' unconscious, dangerous. He's a-lyin' there because the super had an enemy.

"'Where would you get the food you're a-eatin' and the shoes you're a-wearin', if there wasn't a mill to work in? Where would that mill be if it wasn't for the super's money?

"Are there any more enemies in this mill?

"To-morrow mornin', 'said I, an' they knew I meant what I said, 'there'll be two marks agin your names; and one'll tell whether you're a friend or a foe. The time has come. You are dismissed."

"Was every man a friend?" asked Billy, leaning forward eagerly.

"William," answered Thomas Murphy, leaning forward, and punctuating his words with his stiff forefinger, "every one of 'em, William. Every one, to a man."

"I'm glad of that," said Billy. "You were a true friend, Mr. Murphy."

"William," said Thomas Murphy, sitting erect in his chair, "that's what the super said—his very words: 'Thomas Murphy, you're a true friend."

Then Billy gave Thomas Murphy some ice-cream and cakes, and some ginger ale.

The last thing that Thomas Murphy said as he went out the garden gate was "William, when are you a-comin' back to the office? All the men want to see you, William."

Billy didn't answer. He climbed up the steps, and then up the stairs.

When he reached his room he went to the chair by the broad window where he could look at the mountains. He had been wondering himself when he was going back to the office. Every time that he had tried to ask Mr. Prescott, something had seemed to stop him. Why didn't Mr. Prescott talk about it? When was he going home?

That night as Billy lay on the seat in the broad window, he told Mr. Prescott about Tom's speech to the men.

Then Mr. Prescott said: "I think that you and Tom Murphy did something for me, just then, that nobody else could have done. Things were going wrong, and I couldn't stop them."

Billy said quickly, "I didn't do anything."

"You were in the hospital," said Mr. Prescott, "and the men knew why."

They talked on till the room grew dark. Finally Billy said: "Mr. Murphy asked me when I am going back to the office."

For a minute Mr. Prescott didn't say anything. Then he said slowly:

"Billy, while you've been with me, have you ever thought that you would like to stay here all the time?"

Billy waited a moment.

"No, Mr. Prescott," he said slowly.

Mr. Prescott moved uneasily in his chair, but he didn't say anything.

After a little while Billy said: "This is too nice a place for a boy that works."

"See here, Billy Bradford," said Mr. Prescott, sharply, "we'll have none of that! That sounds like William Wallace. He was telling you to let me down easy, was he? You may just as well understand, both of you," he went on, firing his words at Billy in the dark, "you may as well understand, once for all, that you can't tell, simply by looking at the house a man lives in, how hard that man works. Sometimes a man works so hard that he doesn't know what sort of house he does live in. That doesn't mean," he said calming down a little, "that I don't care about this house, for I do. It helps a man to live the right sort of life."

Then he said, still more quietly:

"There's another thing I want you to understand. It's Billy himself that I want. I'm not talking to William Wallace. He is very well able to take care of himself. If I'm not talking to Billy, I'll not talk. Which is it?" he demanded.

"It's Billy," said Billy, very humbly.

"Then give me a true answer, Billy Bradford," he said gently. "It has been very pleasant to have you here, Billy," he went on, almost persuadingly. "When you go I shall be all alone."

Billy waited. He must, in honor, tell the truth. Then his man-side came to help him, and he said slowly:

"Next to Uncle John, I like you better than anybody."

He waited another moment before he finished:

"But my father gave me to my Uncle John."

Mr. Prescott sat still so long that Billy began to wonder whether he was ever going to say anything more.

At last he said: "You do belong to your Uncle John. He has the first right. But I have a right of my own. You've come into my life, and you're not going out of it."

Then Mr. Prescott sat silent so long that Billy wondered, again, whether he ever would say anything more.

Just as Billy had decided that that was the end, Mr. Prescott began slowly, in a sort of far-away tone, as though he hadn't quite come back from a place where he had been off to think:

"I'm going to be your brother, Billy Bradford."

Then he added, in a tone that men like Mr. Prescott use only when they mean things hard:

"Just as long as I live."

Mr. Prescott didn't know it, but he had touched a place in Billy's heart that nobody had ever touched before. Nobody except Billy knew that he had such a place.

Billy waited a minute—a long minute, then he said slowly:

"I've wished and wished and wished that I had a big brother of my own."

"Then," said Mr. Prescott, "your wish has come true."

He said that as though he was as glad as he could be that he had worked that thing out right.

Then, getting up and going over to the nearest electric chain, he said firmly, like the Mr. Prescott that Billy loved best:

"That big brother is right here. His name is Henry Marshall Prescott, and he's here, right here."

CHAPTER XIII

IRON HORSES

OU'VE been kept still so long, Billy Bradford," said Mr. Prescott at breakfast the next Tuesday morning, "that it seems to me it would do you good to move around a little. Think so yourself?"

"Seems that way to me," answered Billy.

"Last night," said Mr. Prescott, "I called up that yellow-haired doctor of yours -"

"Dr. Crandon," interrupted Billy, "is a friend of mine. His hair is only light brown."

"Well then, begging your pardon, Dr. Crandon says he thinks, now that the weather is cooler, a motor trip would do you good. When I asked him whether he would like to go, he said that he would, and that he could start by Thursday. With one on the front seat with Joseph, there's a seat to spare. I've been wondering."

Billy's eyes were so full of wishing that Mr. Prescott asked: "Who is it, Billy?"

"Of course—I don't suppose—I should like—" said Billy

96

floundering around, because he wasn't quite sure how Mr. Prescott would feel about inviting Uncle John.

"You needn't," said Mr. Prescott, "go through the formality of telling me. There's only one person in the world on your mind, Billy Bradford, when your eyes look like that. He's the one I want myself, so you needn't think you've got ahead of me there. The only question is, how shall we manage it? Shall we ask him, or shall we run away with him?"

"Run away with him," said Billy, half in surprise and half in assent.

"Suppose," said Mr. Prescott, "that you go out into the garden this morning, and stay there till you've figured that out."

Then, just as though he were giving an order to one of his men, he added, as he rose from the table:

"You may report to me at noon."

Before the morning was over, Billy had decided that figuring things out was very much harder than going on errands that other people had planned.

He sat in the summer house till he was tired. Then he walked around all the paths. But settle it he would, for Uncle John must never, never lose a chance like that.

Settle it he did, and made his report:

"We could tell him, the night before, that there was something special that I wanted to ask him, and that he could come here at nine o'clock and take his time about getting back to work -"

"That," interrupted Mr. Prescott, "will hit the case exactly. I'll see that he takes his time about getting back."

"And," continued Billy, "I could go to see Aunt Mary this afternoon and tell her about it, and get my bank book -"

"Your what?" demanded Mr. Prescott.

"My bank book. You see Uncle John's blue serge suit will be all right, but he'll need a cap. Aunt Mary has to plan for things like that, so I want my bank book."

"I've been thinking about motor clothes," said Mr. Prescott. "I'll look in that closet at the office. There are some extra things there. I can put some things of mine in the trunk. I wouldn't bother, just now, to draw any money. Know anything about the size of his hat?"

"Yes," answered Billy, "it's only a size smaller than yours. You remember that I looked in yours one day."

"Yes," said Mr. Prescott, "I believe that looking at the size of hats is one of your fads."

"My Uncle John," said Billy, "isn't so very tall, but he has quite a large head."

Billy tried to say it offhand, but his pride showed, all the way through.

"Your Uncle John," said Mr. Prescott, paying very close attention to the chop that he was eating, "is both an unusual man, and an unusually good-looking man."

Perhaps there were two people at that table who could make offhand remarks.

"The next thing," said Mr. Prescott, leaning back in his chair, "is what is to become of your Aunt Mary while your Uncle John is taking his time to return."

"I wisht she could go up in the country," said Billy.

"How would it do for you to find out this afternoon where she would like to go? Then we could talk it over tonight."

So, for the first time since his accident, Billy went back home. It seemed to him that the auto had never run so slowly.

Aunt Mary was very much surprised. She asked him, right off, whether he had come home to stay.

"Not yet," answered Billy.

After he had been into all the rooms, Billy said:

"Aunt Mary, won't you come out to sit on the steps? I want to talk to you."

How good it did seem to be sitting on those steps!

They talked and talked, and Aunt Mary grew very much excited over the trip.

"It'll do him a world of good!" she said. "You don't know how we've both worried about you, Billy."

While she was talking, Billy was watching her; he was trying to decide where her smile left off.

When she said she could manage the part about Uncle John, Billy said:

"Are you sure your face won't give it away?"

"Do I look as glad as that?" she asked, putting her hand up to her face. "No," she went on, "he'll think it's because you have been home."

Billy looked around. The potatoes by the fence had been dug, and Uncle John had smoothed the ground all down again. He wouldn't have been John Bradford if he hadn't done that.

"Home's the best place, isn't it, Aunt Mary?" said Billy, with a little sigh of happiness.

Then he remembered that he must manage Aunt Mary, too. He must try to get around it so that she wouldn't suspect anything. When he thought of the right way, it seemed very simple.

"Aunt Mary," he said, "if you had an automobile, where do you think you would go first?"

That surely ought to throw her off the track, for she could never expect to have an automobile. It surely did throw her off the track.

"Billy," she said, "that's a queer thing to ask me."

Then she said soberly:

"Don't you know, Billy, there's only one place in the world where I should want to go first?"

"Up in the country," said Billy, growing sober, too, "where—where you got me?"

Aunt Mary simply bowed her head.

Wednesday afternoon Mr. Prescott dictated ever so many letters to Miss King. The last was one to Mrs. John Bradford in which Mr. Prescott begged that Mrs. Bradford would be so kind as to make use of the enclosed, so that he might be relieved from concern about her while Mr. Bradford was away with him.

Then Mr. Prescott took from his pocket a ticket that had on it "to" and "return." After the "to" came a name, not very long, on the ticket, but one that, when it reached Aunt Mary's eyes, would read, The Place of Places.

"Here," said Mr. Prescott, "is the enclosure. Please write that letter first, Miss King. That must be posted tonight."

That was Wednesday night. Then Mr. Prescott went home and told Billy that he must go to bed as soon as he had had his supper, so that he would be ready to start in the morning.

Thursday morning came. So did Joseph with the car.

If ever a man looked pleased with himself, it was Mr. Henry Marshall Prescott when he gave his motor coat a final pull with both hands, and settled himself on the seat behind Joseph, with Billy between him and his Uncle John.

They certainly did look well.

The young doctor knew all about automobile "togs," as he called them. So, of course, he was strictly up to date.

There were some other up-to-date "togs" in that car. In point of fact, there were a good many. They had been sent up to the office the day before.

Some of them were Billy's. Being only a boy, he hadn't thought of having any special clothes, but he had on everything that Mr. Prescott had been able to find "for a boy of thirteen." Some of them were Uncle John's. Even Dr. Crandon's weren't any nearer up to calendar time than were those which Mr. Prescott had provided for John Bradford.

When he had helped John Bradford on with the coat, Mr. Prescott had looked straight at Billy with a say-anything-if-you-dare expression.

He knew, just as well as Billy did, that, though he had looked there, those things never came out of the closet at the mill.

When Uncle John put on goggles, Billy's smile changed into a broad grin.

That didn't disturb John Bradford. When he did a thing, he liked to do it all.

That morning, when Billy had told him about the trip and about Aunt Mary, he had taken time enough to smile a long, happy smile. Then he had said:

"Enjoy good things as they come along, and be thankful."

He had worked that motto hard for a great many years, and he was ready to use it again. So he gave himself up to enjoying and to being thankful.

The car was a six-cylinder—a big six, and Joseph was a steady driver.

They had gone about twenty miles when Dr. Crandon said:

"We are going along as smooth as glass."

"I," said John Bradford, "am enjoying the way that we go up-hill. I never could bear to see a horse straining every muscle to pull me up-hill."

"I think," said Mr. Prescott, "that horses ought to be thankful to the men that make automobiles or any sort of iron horse."

Billy looked up at him.

"Iron horses," he said. "I never thought of it that way before. There doesn't seem to be any end to iron."

"How about steel, young chap?" asked Dr. Crandon, from the front seat.

"That's iron," said Billy, "but I don't know much about it except that it makes tools and swords."

"And knives," said Dr. Crandon, way down in his throat.

"Oh!" said Billy.

But nobody knew whether he said it to Dr. Crandon, or whether it was because the car came to a sudden stop.

"Puncture, sir," said Joseph.

However Mr. Prescott may have felt, and he probably did have some feelings, he acted as though he didn't mind in the least.

"That grove looks inviting," he said. "Suppose we have some lunch."

Then he unstrapped the lunch basket and, in a few minutes, they were all sitting under the trees enjoying sandwiches and ginger ale.

"Seems rather pleasant," said Mr. Prescott, "to have a change. Dr. Crandon, what were you saying about knives?"

"Let me see," said Dr. Crandon; "nothing, I think, except that they are made of steel. I'm somewhat interested in the subject."

"Do you," asked Billy, "know where jack-knives first came from?"

"Yes, young chap, I do. I know where some of the best come from now. I've been to Sheffield."

"Where's that?" asked Billy.

"England. You'll often find the name on knives. I bought a steel ink eraser the other day which the clerk told me was 'genuine Sheffield.'

"About the time that Queen Elizabeth died, Sheffield was famous for something else that you could never, never guess."

"What?" asked Billy.

"Jew's harps," answered Dr. Crandon.

"Now, Billy," said Mr. Prescott, "you can add the marks on steel to the sizes of hats."

"I will," said Billy.

"Look for Birmingham," said Uncle John. "That's famous for tools."

"And Toledo is the place for scissors," added Mr. Prescott.

"Speaking of marks," said Dr. Crandon, "I have a sword marked with a crown."

"A genuine Ferrara!" exclaimed Mr. Prescott. "I'm not going to covet my neighbor's goods, but if you should ever come across another, please remember that I have only a Damascus and a Toledo."

"Only!" exclaimed Dr. Crandon. "Those ought to be enough

to satisfy any man. No special virtue in your not coveting my Ferrara."

"The point and the hilt of mine will come together, just the same," he added with boyish pride.

"Bradford," said Mr. Prescott, "you've been keeping pretty still. What's in your mind?"

"Just then," answered John Bradford, "I was thinking about something that my grandfather told me about his father."

"As I figure it," interrupted Mr. Prescott, "he would be Billy's great-great-great-grandfather."

"Yes," replied John Bradford.

Billy, glancing at Mr. Prescott, smiled a satisfied sort of smile.

"He," said John Bradford, "came from Massachusetts. He said that they used to fish up iron out of ponds with tongs such as oyster dredgers use."

"Honest and true!" broke in Billy.

"Fact, Billy. Don't interrupt," said Mr. Prescott, shaking his head at Billy.

"He said," continued John Bradford, "that, many a time, he had fished up half a ton a day."

"That bog ore," said Dr. Crandon, "is very interesting. It is deposited by infusoria–*gaillonella ferruginea*," he added, trying to speak very professionally, though the corners of his mouth were twitching with fun.

Seeing that Billy was regarding him rather critically, he went on:

"You see, young chap, that there is iron almost everywhere; and it is very soluble in water, so it naturally goes into ponds; and those tiny animals in some way make it over into bog ore."

"The senior doctor was talking with me, the other day, about giving you some iron."

"What for?" asked Billy abruptly.

"It's iron in your blood that makes your cheeks red; iron in red apples; iron -"

"Pardon me, doctor," interrupted Mr. Prescott, "the tire is on."

"By the way, Bradford, I believe you've been told to take your time about returning?"

"So I understand," answered John Bradford, smiling as he spoke.

"Then, if you don't mind, Bradford, we'll motor on to a place where these young fellows," he said, waving his hand toward the doctor and Billy, "may be able to learn a thing or two more on the subject of iron."

CHAPTER XIV

THE GIANTS

HEY stood on the dock of a river where great ships leave their burden of iron ore.

"There she comes!" exclaimed Mr. Prescott, pointing to a freighter that was slowly drawing near.

"No giants in sight yet," said Billy.

"It's your eyes that are not seeing," returned Mr. Prescott. "That boat herself is a giantess. Watch."

Hardly had the great boat been made fast to her moorings before, in some mysterious way, the hold of the ship opened wide from stem to stern. Then somebody touched a lever somewhere, and over the hold swung a row of buckets that, opening like two hands, grabbed into the ore, and seizing tons of it, swung back to the dock. A touch of another lever unloaded it into huge storage bins.

"Billy Bradford," said Mr. Prescott, "weren't those the hands of a giant?"

"Sure, sir," answered Billy, who stood staring in wonder.

"That ore," said Mr. Prescott, "came from a surface mine

106

up in the pine woods of Lake Superior, a thousand miles away. Perhaps, gentlemen, you may like to know that the American supremacy in iron is largely due to those open pit mines up in Minnesota. Much of the ore in that region is so near the surface that a steam shovel can easily strip off the 'overburden' of the soil and the roots of pine trees. When that was done, giant hands seized that ore, lifted it up, and loaded it into bins, high up on the bluffs. Then a man, not a giant, touched a treadle, and another kind of giant, named 'gravity,' made the ore run from the bottom of the car into a bin. Chutes from the ore bin ran into the hold of the steamer, and almost before she had been tied to the dock she was ready to come down here. Giants or not, Billy Bradford?"

"Iron giants," answered Billy.

"Rather different, Mr. Bradford," said Dr. Crandon, "from fishing ore with tongs."

"We've moved along a great way since that time," said John Bradford, "and most of our progress has been due to iron."

"Giants don't do all the work even now," said Mr. Prescott. "They make short work of iron mountains and surface deposits, but most of them are too large to work underground; though we mustn't forget that Giant Electricity works down there with the men. Giant Gravity helps too, for, when they work below the deposit, he caves the ore down. Of course some ores are so hard that they can't be caved, so there is still some mining for the men to do."

"Was there," asked Billy, trying to speak in a sort of offhand way, "an iron mountain where this iron came from?"

"There are some," answered Mr. Prescott, "up in that region."

Billy had been paying very close attention to what Mr. Prescott had been saying. There was something that he wanted especially to find out. He felt very sure, now, that he was hearing about an iron mountain that he had heard about once before. He felt very sure, but he wouldn't ask any more questions, because that was the secret that he had with Thomas Murphy.

The others started for the car. But Billy stood a moment longer to look at the giant hands that, having finished their work, were hanging idly in the air. The hold of the ship, emptied of its burden, was already beginning to close.

"Beginning to believe in giants, aren't you?" said Mr. Prescott, as Billy stepped into the car.

The next giant will be a hungry fellow, and he is very, very tall; so he eats a great deal.

"An iron-eater, is he?" queried Dr. Crandon.

"We ourselves will have something to eat before we visit him," said Mr. Prescott, ordering Joseph to drive back to the hotel.

"Mr. Prescott," said Dr. Crandon, as they sat at table, "is iron ever found in a pure state, like gold, for instance?"

"It is practically never found in a pure state," answered Mr. Prescott, "except the meteoric iron, 'the stone of heaven.'"

Billy looked at him questioningly.

"That was rather technical, wasn't it, Billy? You see, I was talking to a technical man. Just between you and me, meteoric iron comes down from the sky, from what we call shooting stars. Sometimes large pieces are found. I suppose that much of it falls into the sea. It is the purest iron that has ever been found."

"What about magnetic iron?" asked Dr. Crandon. "Where does that come from?"

"At the present time," answered Mr. Prescott, "most of it comes from Sweden and Norway. It makes the best kind of steel. Ages ago, the first was found in Magnesia," said Mr. Prescott casting a quick glance around the table. "The people there found certain hard, black stones which would attract to themselves bits of iron and steel. So they named them magnets, from Magnesia, the place where the stones were found," finished Mr. Prescott, with another look around the table.

"It's of no use, Prescott," said Dr. Crandon, "you needn't look at us. We don't any of us know even where to look for Magnesia. Don't suppose we could find it even if we had a map."

"I presume you remember, Crandon," said Mr. Prescott, "the place that boasted that ancient wonder of the world, the Temple of Diana."

"Ephesus!" said Dr. Crandon, quickly. "I do happen to know that Ephesus is in Asia Minor."

"Then," said Mr. Prescott, still keeping his face very grave, "I should strongly advise your finding Ephesus first. That's in the near neighborhood of Magnesia."

"Thank you," said Dr. Crandon gravely. "Though I did not know where magnetic iron came from, I do happen to know that it is sometimes called 'lode-stone.' And I know, too, that Sir Isaac Newton—he's the one, Billy, who ran down Giant Gravity—had a ring set with a lode-stone that could lift two hundred and fifty times its own weight."

"And I know," said Mr. Prescott, "that I am very grateful to Dr. Crandon for telling me about the new electro-magnet that I now have at the mill. I feel very much easier, now, about my workmen's eyes."

"Do you mean," asked Billy, "that thing that you brought home that I thought was a new desk telephone?"

"It does resemble a telephone," said Dr. Crandon, "only it has a tip instead of a mouthpiece. It's a great thing for taking bits of steel out of eyes."

"Isn't there such a thing," asked John Bradford, "as a magnetic separator?"

"Glad to hear from you once more, Bradford," said Mr. Prescott, with a smile. "It has been some time since you have said anything."

"I have been having too good a time," said John Bradford, "to want to talk. I should like, now, to have you tell us about the separator."

"It is an electro-magnetic drum. When the finely crushed ore is poured on it in a stream, the drum attracts the iron, while the earthy matter, which is non-magnetic, falls off by the action of gravity. The iron is carried on by the drum, until a brush arrangement sweeps it off into a truck. That is a case, Billy, where Giant Gravity and Giant Electro-magnet fight over the ore, and each gets away with a part of it. Perhaps I ought to explain to you that, when a bar of soft iron is put inside an insulated coil of copper wire and a current of electricity is passed through it, it becomes a powerful magnet. That is what we mean by an electro-magnet. The advantage of that is that it ceases to be a magnet when the current ceases, so it can be controlled. You will see some before I am through showing you giants. There is also an electric cleaner that collects the iron that is left in the corners of cars. Those devices save iron. Strange as it may seem, however, not all iron will respond to the magnetic cleaners."

"Is there," asked Dr. Crandon, "any danger that the iron in the world will be exhausted?"

"I hardly think so," answered Mr. Prescott. "The available ores, in the single range that we were talking about this morning, run up into the trillions of metric tons."

"I read something the other day," said John Bradford, "about some iron that had been found in Sweden, up beyond the Arctic Circle."

"That," said Mr. Prescott, "is one of the most extensive deposits in the world. The countries of the western part of Europe draw upon that supply. It is very likely that we haven't found all the iron yet, and even more likely that we shall find a way to make use of the poorer ores. By the way, Billy, there is one kind of iron called 'iron pyrites.' It looks so much like gold that it has deceived many a poor fellow into thinking that he had found gold. It well deserves the name 'fool's gold.' It doesn't even make good iron. I'll show you some when we go home. Now we'll go to see the iron-eater."

Ten minutes later Billy exclaimed:

"He's tall!"

"Not quite a hundred feet," said Mr. Prescott.

"He's black!" said Dr. Crandon.

"He roars!" added John Bradford.

"And," said Mr. Prescott, "even if he could be moved, he's rather too valuable for a circus manager to buy, for he cost a million dollars. I really think he's the most fearful thing ever made by man. The Germans, though, did a great thing for iron when they evolved the blast furnace."

"The Most Fearful Thing Ever Made"

"Makes our cupola," said John Bradford, as they stopped before the tall iron stack, "look very small."

"Ours," said Mr. Prescott, "is only a dwarf, but he does something the same work; only here they put in iron ore instead of pig iron. Blast furnaces make pig iron."

"What diet," asked Dr. Crandon, "do they give this giant?"

"You're bound to think professionally, aren't you, Crandon? He's restricted to coke, iron ore, and limestone, but they feed him very often. They see, too, that he has plenty of hot air to breathe. The old problem used to be how to get heat enough to melt the ore. That was solved by a Scotchman, who originated the use of the hot blast. The gas produced by the furnace used to be wasted. Now they utilize it in the hot-blast stoves. That accounts for some of the huge pipes attached to the furnace. Come this way, and I'll show you a stove.

"Here it is, almost as tall as the furnace itself. This giant, also, is encased in an armor of iron plates. If we could look inside, we should see that it is almost filled with open brick work that resembles a honeycomb. They send hot gas over the brick work till the stove is hot, then they shut off the gas and start the engine that blows in cold air. That, heated by the bricks, is forced into the furnace. One of those great pipes up there is where they draw off the slag. It is so much lighter than the iron that it rises to the top, like cream on milk. Down here they draw off the iron. Sometimes they keep it hot for the next process; sometimes it is made into pig iron."

"What," asked Dr. Crandon, "becomes of the slag?"

"That depends somewhat on the chemical composition of the slag. Some kinds are broken up to be used as foundation for roads; others are granulated by being run into water, and so made into cement. Over in Germany, where the ores are rich in phosphorus, they grind up the linings of the furnace to make phosphatic fertilizers for the farmers."

"Then," said Dr. Crandon, "the making of iron involves the use of chemistry, doesn't it?"

"It certainly does," answered Mr. Prescott; "from the chemical composition of ores to the finished product. We are learning a great deal just now from the chemists about steel alloys. I didn't tell you that from the gas they sometimes save ammonia, tar, and oils, before it is fed to the hot-blast stoves."

"By-products," said Dr. Crandon, "seem to be a feature of modern industry."

"It is high time," said Mr. Prescott, "that waste should receive attention. Before we leave this giant I must tell you that he already has a dangerous rival—listen, Billy, for it's almost a David and Goliath story—in a little electric smelter. Some of them can be moved about like a portable sawmill. Up in Sweden, where the ores are among the purest in the world, they use electric smelters and make steel direct from the ore."

"Any more giants?" asked Billy.

"You'll think so," answered Mr. Prescott, "before I am through with them; but we've seen enough for to-day. Next time I'll show you giants that have done something more than to make iron, for they have really reduced the size of the world."

"Whew!" exclaimed Dr. Crandon.

"Before that," said Mr. Prescott, "I am going to introduce you to some pygmies."

CHAPTER XV

THE PYGMIES

"SHALL we need glasses, Prescott, in order to see your pygmies?" asked Dr. Crandon, the next morning, while they were waiting for the car.

"I will agree to furnish all the glasses needed," answered Mr. Prescott.

Much as Billy wanted to know what Mr. Prescott was going to show them, he had made up his mind to trust to his eyes to find out.

John Bradford was learning so many things that he had long wanted to know that he was simply enjoying things as they came along, and being thankful.

"To the office of the steel works, Joseph," said Mr. Prescott.

On past the great yard of the blast furnace they went, then along by some high brick walls until they stopped in front of a two-story cement building.

Then they followed Mr. Prescott till he stopped at the head of the stairs, and knocked at a door.

"Come in," shouted somebody in a cordial voice.

115

"Hullo, Harry, old fellow!" said the owner of the voice, still more cordially, as he came forward with outstretched hand.

"This," said Mr. Prescott, "is my classmate, Mr. Farnsworth, who is at the head of the laboratory."

After he had introduced John Bradford and Dr. Crandon, he added, "And this is Billy Bradford."

Then he said, "I've brought these friends of mine to see your show. We've been to see some of the giants in the iron industry. Now I want them to have a look at your pygmies."

"Pygmies they shall see," said Mr. Farnsworth, with an appreciative smile. "Hardly a technical term, but a good way, Harry, to get hold of the facts. Pygmies they shall be.

"Sit down, all of you," he said, pointing to chairs by his low, broad table.

Pushing back the sliding door of a case behind the table, he took out a tray containing small round pieces of iron and steel.

"Shall I tell you about these specimens, or will you ask me?"

"Just give us a general idea, Jack," answered Mr. Prescott; "we might ask the wrong questions."

"Then, Billy Bradford," said Mr. Farnsworth, smiling at Billy, "I'll explain to you, and the others may listen.

"You see we chemists analyze the ores before they are smelted; so we know something about what kind of pig iron we shall have. But when we want to know what kind of finished iron or steel we have from a given process, we can't tell much by analyzing it, so we have to depend on our microscopes.

"Metals crystallize, if they have just the right conditions. Each metal has its own form; so, if you could find a single crystal, you would recognize it by its form.

"But when melted iron grows solid, the crystals are crowded so close together that, when it is prepared for the microscope, and polished like this, the surface looks as if it were made up of crystal grains.

"Sometimes crystallization takes place in steel if it is subjected to long repeated jar. Many accidents in engines are due to that."

As he took the cover off his microscope, Mr. Farnsworth said:

"I suppose, Harry, that your 'pygmies' are the elements that are found in the various kinds of iron?"

"The same," answered Mr. Prescott.

"Then I shall tell Billy Bradford that some of the pygmies are enemies and others are friends; some need to be driven away, and others should be invited to come in.

"The most numerous enemies are the carbon pygmies. The blast furnace drives most of them off, but they have to be fought in the pig iron, too.

"Sulphur pygmies are about the worst of all, because they make the iron brittle. They are practically the hardest to drive away.

"Phosphorus pygmies haven't a good reputation, but they are in much better standing than the Sulphur enemies.

"Now, if you'll look in here—this is the purest and the softest Swedish bar iron—you'll see where the edges of the crystals come together. These are friendly Ferrite pygmies, crowding close together. Ferrum is the Latin name for iron; you must remember that."

"If I didn't know," said John Bradford, when he took his turn, "I should think I was looking at some sort of wood with a very fine grain."

"This," said Mr. Farnsworth, changing the specimen, "has black and white streaks in it; that means that the iron has begun to be steel. When it has light patches like these in it, we know that it has taken up more carbon, and has grown harder.

"So it goes," he said, showing one after another of the specimens. "You can see for yourself that, if friendly pygmies stand in line, taking hold of hands, that would make a good kind of iron to draw out into a wire. If enemies stand around in groups, they make the iron easy to break.

"When we want steel for chisels, for example, we invite Tungsten to come in; when we want certain parts for automobiles we call in some Vanadium pygmies."

"So," said Mr. Prescott, "while we need the giants to make the pig iron, the real value of the iron and steel depends on the pygmies."

"That's about the size of it," said Mr. Farnsworth.

"Anything the trouble with you, young chap?" asked Dr. Crandon. "You haven't spoken for ten minutes. Feel bad anywhere?"

"No," answered Billy. "I was just wishing I could know about all those things."

"I'm glad it's nothing worse than that," said Dr. Crandon.

"Now," said Mr. Prescott, "we'll start for some more giants. Coming, Farnsworth?"

"Sorry, not to-day. Call again!"

"The steel mill comes next on my program," said Mr. Prescott, when they went out. "I want you to see a Bessemer converter, an open hearth, and some crucibles, because that practically covers the different methods of making iron and steel. Here is the Bessemer converter. You see it is an iron cylinder made of wrought iron plates, and it tapers off at the top in a conical end. See. It is swinging down to be filled almost as easily as you can turn your hand over. In a moment it will stand up again, twenty-five feet tall.

"Bessemer got hold of the idea that air could be used instead of fuel. They say he risked his life in his experiments. He worked a long time, but he won, and the Bessemer converters started the boom in steel.

"See it come up again, with fifteen tons of hot pig iron in it. Down in the bottom of the converter is a blast chest where the air is forced in under pressure, after it has been blown into a tank by blowing engines."

"O-o-oh!" exclaimed Billy, as the top of the converter seemed to burst into flame, and a shower of sparks came down.

"That," said Dr. Crandon, "is surely a fearful sort of thing!"

Then the flame began to drop slowly, and they saw that the converter itself was safe.

"This process burns out all the carbon. Bessemer was trying to make wrought iron when he started out. Now they put back the right amount of carbon, and make the iron into steel.

"It's a chemical process. When the air strikes the hot metals the oxygen unites with them, and they burst into flame. The whole process takes between fifteen and twenty minutes."

"I am very sure," said Dr. Crandon, "that I shouldn't like to work here."

"When we get to the open hearth process, which is the rival of the Bessemer," said Mr. Prescott, "I expect that none of you will want to work there."

"For my part," said John Bradford, slowly, "I prefer Prescott mill."

"So do I," said Billy.

"Which reminds me," said Mr. Prescott, "to tell you that I have been looking at some machines to help in the foundry. They will help about lifting and ramming; but they won't do away with the work of men.

"Here we are, gentlemen, before a Siemens-Martin open hearth. This is a continuous process. It was evolved by Sir William Siemens, a German-English engineer, and his brother. Then a man named Martin, a Frenchman, I understand, found a way to mix the iron and steel that are put on the hearth, so it bears both the names.

"We'll just look in. It is a large, shallow basin, made of bricks, partly filled with iron. Both hot air and gas are burned on top of the iron. The process takes seven or eight hours; but it produces larger quantities of steel than the Bessemer converters can do.

"Then, too, it furnishes all kinds of iron and steel, for they sample it as it burns, and draw off the steel at any percentage of carbon that they want.

"Cast iron has a great deal of carbon in it; steel has much less; and wrought iron has almost none.

"Now, we'll go over to the crucible furnace."

They walked slowly across the yard.

"There are no giants here," said Mr. Prescott, "with the exception of the furnaces in which they set the crucibles; and they are small, compared with the furnaces that we have seen."

They found themselves in a long room lined with shelves of clay crucibles, about eighteen inches in height. On the sides of the room, under the shelves, were rows of small furnaces, each large enough for two crucibles.

"The crucible process," said Mr. Prescott, "gives us our finest steels. It is a simple melting together of iron and charcoal. The carbon of the charcoal passes into the iron. When the crucibles are filled, they are set in the furnace, and left for several days.

"They make a special kind of crucible steel over in Sheffield."

While he was saying that, Mr. Prescott glanced at Billy, but Billy was looking at the furnace, and did not hear what Mr. Prescott said.

Mr. Prescott looked at him hard, as he said:

"The home of the crucible is Sheffield."

"Sheffield," said Billy, turning, "is where they make good jack-knives."

"Want to see a genuine Sheffield?" asked Mr. Prescott, putting his hand into his pocket.

That time he didn't have to attract Billy's attention, for Billy stood waiting.

"See," said Mr. Prescott, pulling out a chain that had a knife on it, and opening the blades. "See, it has Sheffield on both blades."

Billy's eyes saw the "Sheffield." Then they saw something else, for on the side of the knife was a little silver plate, and on it—he had to look twice—was "Billy Bradford."

"That's a good knife," said Billy.

The three men smiled, each his very best smile.

"Thank you, Mr. Prescott," said Billy as he took the knife. Then he smiled, too.

"Now for the steel mill, and the last of our giants."

"Is the mill deserted?" asked Dr. Crandon, as they went in.

"It's much easier," said Mr. Prescott, "to find the giants

in a steel mill than it is to find the men. If you look around you'll find a few, but they'll be in most unexpected places."

"I see a man," exclaimed Billy, "up in a cage!"

"He's controlling that crane," said Mr. Prescott. "See it carry that ingot of red-hot iron!"

"This," said Dr. Crandon, "passes belief. There's a boy over there, in a reclining chair, who is opening a furnace down on this side."

"Look at that!" exclaimed John Bradford, pointing to a crane like a huge thumb and forefinger, which had picked up a red-hot ingot, tons in weight, and was dropping it on a waiting car.

"Let's follow it," said Mr. Prescott, pleased to see John Bradford so excited.

They followed it to a room filled with clanking rolls.

Another crane swung the red-hot iron into the jaws of rollers.

On went the fiery bolt, sometimes up on one roller, then down on another, till at last they found that it had come out a finished rail.

Then a huge, round steel magnet, lowered by a man in a derrick house, picked up half a dozen rails; another lever sent the crane down the overhead tracks; and the rails were dropped in order on waiting cars.

"It used," said Mr. Prescott, "to take a dozen men to load a single rail.

"Giants or not, Billy Bradford?"

"Giants for sure," replied Billy.

"Fire-eaters!" exclaimed Dr. Crandon. "Let's go!"

"I'm ready," said Mr. Prescott. "I'm glad that the work is

so much easier for the men, but I must confess that I don't care to watch red-hot iron shooting, almost flying around."

"I'm ready to go," said Billy.

"Joseph," said Mr. Prescott, a few minutes later, "drive till you find a country road."

That evening, as they sat together on the hotel veranda, Mr. Prescott said:

"I've been thinking," then he stopped a moment to see whether Billy was listening, "how much iron has done to make the world smaller."

Then, seeing that Billy's eyes were opening wider and wider, he said:

"The world is so much smaller than it used to be that I sometimes wonder how much smaller it may grow."

"Isn't it just as far around the world as it always was?" asked Billy, looking first at Mr. Prescott, then at his Uncle John, and then back at Mr. Prescott.

"It's of no use, Billy," said Dr. Crandon, "to expect this man to tell us anything straight out. He's trying to train our minds. If we're going around with him, we shall have to submit to indirect methods of obtaining information."

"If you'll excuse me, Crandon," said Mr. Prescott, "I'm not sure that Billy won't learn as fast by my 'indirect methods' as he will by the kind of words that you are using."

"Even, I think," said Dr. Crandon.

Then the three men smiled, each in his own way.

Billy didn't smile. All his best heroes seemed to be showing "disagreeable spots" at the same time.

But Billy had only a minute of thinking that, for Dr. Crandon said, in his most friendly tone:

"I think I know what he's driving at, so I'll lend you a hand. It would take a long time to sail around the world, wouldn't it?"

"Sure," answered Billy, quite like himself.

"But, if we were to start in an automobile, and drive to a train that would take us to San Francisco -"

"And then," said Uncle John, "take a steamer across the ocean -"

"And," finished Mr. Prescott, "get back home in less than forty days, wouldn't that make the world smaller than if we had to sail and sail and sail?"

"Of course," answered Billy. "Anybody can see that."

"And, if you were to go alone, Billy," continued Mr. Prescott, in his very friendliest tone, "you could wire me or 'phone me or cable me almost anywhere along the route. Wouldn't that make the world seem very small?

"And what do all these things mean but iron—iron engines and iron rails and iron wires and watches with steel springs and magnetic steel needles in compasses that guide the great steamers through the paths of the sea?"

"Sometimes," said Billy, in a half-discouraged tone, "I think there's no end to knowing about iron."

"That's not very far from true, Billy," said Mr. Prescott. "We could sit here till to-morrow morning trying to mention things made of iron, or by means of iron, and then we should be likely to forget many of them.

"If it weren't for iron and steel implements and tools, men would have hard work to earn a living.

"Dr. Crandon, what does it seem to you that we should lose if we were to lose iron?"

"I've been thinking about the arts—surgery, too. We need

iron for sculpture, for music, for printing books and papers. We need iron, I should say, for art's sake."

"And you, Bradford?"

"I've been thinking about agriculture. I never realized, before this trip, how we really depend on iron for our food. That phosphatic fertilizer set me to thinking about plows, mills, and all sorts of things."

"I think," said Mr. Prescott, "that the man was right who said that the strength of nations depends on coal and iron far more than it does on gold.

"Another man said practically the same when he said that iron has given man liberty and industry: tools and implements of peace, as well as weapons of war. When you think it out, that seems to cover it all.

"Now, Billy," Mr. Prescott went on, "I know what you will say. You may say it."

"Without iron," said Billy, smiling up at Mr. Prescott, "we should be just 'nothin', nobody.'"

"My lecture course," said Mr. Prescott, "is now finished.

"To-morrow, I am going to show you where they try to make—do make—something greater than iron."

CHAPTER XVI

WHAT MR. PRESCOTT SAID

"A T four o'clock, Joseph."

Billy looked at Mr. Prescott wonderingly.

"Why four o'clock, questioner? Because, when I'm going to see a place, I like to see it at its best. I like to see this place in the afternoon, when the shadows have grown long. No; no more questions."

At a quarter past four, Joseph stopped the car in front of a beautiful wrought iron gate.

"That's a beauty!" exclaimed Dr. Crandon. "It reminds me of some of the old medieval work that I saw in Italy. What's this, anyway?"

Mr. Prescott shook his head.

"All right, Prescott," said Dr. Crandon, "I'll wait."

"As for that gate," said Mr. Prescott, "I may as well admit that I am a bit proud of it. The men of my year put it there.

"As for the place, I think," said Mr. Prescott slowly, "I think I might safely say that it is where they make, or try to make, a certain kind of castings."

126

"Would it be fair, Prescott," said Dr. Crandon with a smile, "for me to say that you yourself are prone to think professionally?"

"Quite fair, I assure you," answered Mr. Prescott, with a bow.

"I don't see anybody making anything," said Billy, in a disappointed tone.

"In the summer they have to rest both their machinery and their material," said Mr. Prescott.

Then Billy knew that Mr. Prescott expected him to keep his eyes and his ears open until he found out for himself where they were.

"Let's walk," said Mr. Prescott.

They were at the first corner when Billy exclaimed:

"Where's Uncle John?"

"There he is," said Mr. Prescott, turning around. "He's still looking at that gate. Don't blame him much," he added.

Back Billy went.

John Bradford was so absorbed in studying the gate that Billy had to call him the second time before he turned.

"Eh! Billy, my lad!" he said. "I should like to do a piece of work as beautiful as that. That is true artist work."

Something in his tone made Billy say quickly:

"You're an artist yourself, Uncle John. Miss King said so."

"I should really like," said John Bradford again, "to do such a piece of work as that."

"When we get home," said Billy, "why don't you begin?"

"Eh! Billy, my lad!" said Uncle John, but this time he said it with a smile.

"He was wishing," said Billy when they overtook the others, "that he could make an iron gate."

"HE'S STILL LOOKING AT THE GATE"

"I'll confess, here and now," said Mr. Prescott, "that I myself have had aspirations of that sort."

"Is iron-work coming in again?" asked Dr. Crandon. "It seems to me that, just lately, I have seen some very beautiful gates."

"I think so," answered Mr. Prescott. "There are a few men who seem to have caught the spirit of the old smiths, and to have seen the possibilities in wrought iron. The man who made that gate is one of them. He has invented a liquid, too, to prevent the rusting of the iron.

"You see that a man who works in iron must be both an artist and a smith—he must blow the forge and use the hammer. That gate in cast iron would be almost ugly. In the Swedish wrought iron, it is truly beautiful.

"The old fellows knew much more about the artistic side of iron than we do. Look at the old French locks—even a French king prided himself on his ability to make locks.

"There was a time when an apprentice to a locksmith had to make a masterpiece lock before he could become a master. It usually took him two years to do it, for he had to chase and chisel it from the solid.

"I'll tell you, Bradford, something that Billy Bradford doesn't know. I have a workshop of my own at home in the lower part of the house.

"A long time ago I began an iron gate for the garden. When we go back, Bradford, let's finish it."

Billy, looking at his Uncle John, smiled serenely.

Then Billy walked by Uncle John, while Mr. Prescott and Dr. Crandon went slowly before them down the long avenue of elms.

Billy listened to the two men as they talked. He found out that they had both been to college, and then somewhere else. He couldn't quite make out what Mr. Prescott's other place was; but it was somewhere specially to study iron.

This talk about college was all new to Billy. He liked the stories that they told, one after another. He had never seen Mr. Prescott so happy.

"That," he said, stopping before a large brick building that looked very old, "is where I used to room. Second story front.

"Billy, look back."

Billy, turning, saw the great yard, green everywhere, with long shadows of trees and buildings resting on it in the low light of the afternoon.

"It's like the city and the country put together," he said. "It's the most beautiful place that I ever saw!"

"Prescott," said Dr. Crandon, "were you ever on a football team?"

"He was captain," broke in Billy. "He told me so!"

"He's captain still," said John Bradford, in his slow, even way.

They all looked at him a moment.

"Good, Bradford, good!" exclaimed Dr. Crandon. "That's what he is! I'm inclined to think that football is a good training place for a captain of industry."

"It's all team work," said John Bradford. "Some do one thing and some another, but without a captain a team can't win."

There were times when Uncle John said things that Billy couldn't understand. He did just then. But Billy knew, by the look that came into Mr. Prescott's face, that he was very much pleased.

"It takes," said Dr. Crandon, "two sets of men to make the world move along: those who work with their heads, and those who work with their hands. For my part, I believe that one set works about as hard as the other."

"I'm truly thankful, Crandon," said Mr. Prescott, "that there's somebody in the world who realizes that."

Then they all started down the avenue of elms. Mr. Prescott had slipped his arm through John Bradford's, and was talking to him earnestly.

Dr. Crandon and Billy loitered along behind.

"Mr. Prescott seems to be unusually fond of his 'Alma Mater,'" said Dr. Crandon.

"What," asked Billy, "does 'Alma Mater' mean?"

"It's a Latin name for a college," answered Dr. Crandon. "I think that 'cherishing mother' is a pretty good way to translate it into English.

"A college looks after you, and tries to make a man of you, something the way your mother does, you know."

"All the mother I ever had," said Billy, "was only a week."

"Oh, young chap, I'm sorry," said Dr. Crandon, throwing his arm across Billy's shoulder the way college boys sometimes do.

"I tell you what I'd do," he added quickly, "I'd begin to think about an 'Alma Mater.' You could work your way through, you know. I began that way myself.

"Don't you do it, though, on less than three meals a day—square ones," he added with professional zeal.

"I shall keep an eye on you, young chap. I surely shall!"

Then he remembered that he had some letters to post, and hurried off to the nearest box.

Billy kept on walking toward Mr. Prescott and Uncle John, who were coming slowly back under the beautiful trees.

After he had gone a little way, Billy waited, in the middle of the walk, for them to come up.

Mr. Prescott still had his hand through Uncle John's arm. How happy Uncle John looked, and Mr. Prescott, too!

When they reached him, they stopped.

"I've found out," said Billy. "This is where they make—"

"Try to make," corrected Mr. Prescott.

"Men," finished Billy.

Then Mr. Prescott put his hand on Billy's shoulder, and, looking right down into Billy's eyes, said slowly:

"He's your boy, Bradford, but he belongs to me, too.

"We'll work together, and we'll see whether between us we can help him to come to be a man."

www.ingramcontent.com/pod-product-compliance
Lightning Source LLC
Chambersburg PA
CBHW051707180726
48283CB00004B/1241